Amanda waited tensely for Malory to reach for her...

But he didn't. After an endless silence, he spoke, his tone matter-of-fact. "I'll ring you in a few days. Now I'd better see you safely indoors."

Moments later Amanda's hand shook as she fitted her key into the lock. "Thank you for dinner, the flowers...the ring," she said nervously.

Malory put a finger under her chin, tilting her face to meet his gaze. "Calm down...darling. There's nothing to be afraid of." Then he turned and walked back to his car.

Amanda leaned against her closed door, trying to still her rapid breathing. He was perfectly correct. There had been nothing to fear.

She should have felt relief. Why, then, did she somehow feel disappointed?

SARA CRAVEN probably had the ideal upbringing for a budding writer. She grew up by the seaside in a house crammed with books, with a box of old clothes to dress up in and a swing outside in a walled garden. She produced the opening of her first book at age five and is eternally grateful to her mother for having kept a straight face. Now she has more than twenty-five novels to her credit. The author is married and has two children.

Books by Sara Craven

Don't miss any of our special offers. Write to us at the following address for information on our newest releases.

Harlequin Reader Service
901 Fuhrmann Blvd., P.O. Box 1397, Buffalo, NY 14240
Canadian address: P.O. Box 603,
Fort Erie, Ont. L2A 5X3

SARA CRAVEN

comparative strangers

Harlequin Books

TORONTO • NEW YORK • LONDON
AMSTERDAM • PARIS • SYDNEY • HAMBURG
STOCKHOLM • ATHENS • TOKYO • MILAN

Harlequin Presents first edition November 1988
ISBN 0-373-11119-3

Original hardcover edition published in 1988
by Mills & Boon Limited

CHAPTER ONE

IT HAD rained during the week, and the river was in spate, crashing between its banks and hurling itself at the stone bridge as if it sought to sweep it away.

A torn-off branch from some tree came whirling downstream, carried helplessly along by the angry brown waters. From her vantage point on the bridge, Amanda watched as it submerged, drawn down by some unseen vortex, and her hands tightened on the stones of the parapet until the knuckles turned white.

A few seconds, said the small cold voice in her head, and then—oblivion. No more hurting. No more betrayal, cutting at you like a knife, slashing away at all that was warm and joyous and trusting in your life. Nothing.

The rush of the water, the roar of the wind in the trees, seemed to fill her head like a scream of outrage at the life which had turned against her.

She lifted her foot, searching for a hole, feeling the rough surface of the bridge ripping at her fragile tights, scraping her legs. Panting, she dragged herself up on to the parapet and crouched for a moment, closing her eyes against the swift giddiness which assailed her.

She thought, ridiculously, I hate heights.

Slowly, gingerly, she uncurled herself, and stood up. One step was all that she needed to take, she told herself, swaying slightly. Or perhaps the force of the wind would do it for her.

She felt herself lifted, snatched, and she screamed aloud as she realised she was falling, not forward towards the water, but back on to the bridge again.

From a thousand miles away, a man's voice, drawling and vaguely familiar, said, 'It isn't as simple as that, believe me.'

She said a name in anguished disbelief, but it was lost in the inner tumult consuming her, overwhelming her, and consigning her at last to the dark forgetfulness she had sought.

She opened her eyes dazedly to movement and the noise of a car engine, found that she felt deathly sick, and closed her lids hastily.

Later, she became dimly aware of voices in the distance, and of the softness of cushions beneath her. The same familiar voice said, 'Drink this,' and she drank obediently, too weary to protest. Whatever liquid it was, it seemed to run down her throat like fire, but it dissolved away the last of her resistance, and she slept.

She woke to lamplight and firelight, and lay for a few puzzled moments, coming to terms with the fact that she was at home, lying on the sofa in her mother's drawing-room.

She thought, drowsily, But I went to Calthorpe to be with Nigel. How did I get back here?

Memory hit her like a blow, and she sat up with a little stifled cry, her shocked eyes meeting the cool, level gaze of the man who sat on the opposite side of the fireplace.

She said, 'You——Oh God, you...' Then her voice broke, and she began to cry, her body shaking under the impact of deep, gulping sobs.

'Why did you stop me?' she wailed between paroxysms. 'Why the hell did you stop me?'

He got up silently, handed her an immaculate white handkerchief from his breast pocket, and vanished.

Amanda buried her head in the cushions and wept until she had no more tears left. When she eventually lifted her head, he had come back into the room and was putting down a tray, laden with tea things, on to a table in front of her.

He said, conversationally, 'They say tea is the best thing for shock. I wonder if it's true?'

She said huskily, 'I don't want any bloody tea! What are you *doing* here, Malory?'

'I followed you from Calthorpe,' he said. 'I had a feeling you were contemplating something foolish, and I thought I should stop you. That's all.'

'All?' she echoed bitterly. 'Didn't it occur to you to mind your own business?'

'You're engaged to my younger brother,' he said. 'I felt that gave me—a kind of responsibility.'

'Your half-brother.'

'If you want to split hairs.'

'And I'm no longer engaged to him.'

'So I infer.'

It was that coolly precise way of speaking which had so often needled her about Malory. She supposed it came from a lifetime of analysing things

in those damned laboratories of his. But she wasn't
a substance under his bloody microscope—and how
dared he be so calm and matter of fact when he
knew quite well her heart was breaking?

He poured out some tea and handed it to her.
She would have liked to have thrown it over him,
to see if that would ruffle that distant poise of his,
but instead she sipped the hot brew, watching him
sulkily over the rim of her cup. This was only the
second time he'd been to the cottage, she realised,
and he'd lost no time in finding his way around the
kitchen.

She said, frowning, 'How did we get in here,
anyway?' Her keys, she remembered painfully, were
in the car, parked at the bridge.

'Luckily, your cleaning woman was still here,' he
said. 'I told her you weren't feeling well, and I'd
brought you home. I also said I'd stay with you
until your mother returned.'

'Then you'll have a long wait,' she said child-
ishly. 'Mother's in London staying with a friend.
That's why...' She stopped abruptly.

That was why I went to Calthorpe—to be with
Nigel. Because it seemed prudish—ridiculous in this
day and age—to hold back any longer, with the
wedding so close now. Because I didn't want any
more rows—any more accusations about being im-
possibly old-fashioned, or not loving him enough
to trust him.

But that wasn't something she could confide in
Malory, or anyone else, for that matter.

She thought of her mother, happily shopping for
something to wear for her important role as mother

of the bride, and felt another wellspring of grief rising inside her. Damming it back, she drank some more tea.

Malory said gravely, 'You probably wouldn't have drowned, you know. Just injured yourself quite badly.'

'I can't swim,' she returned defiantly.

'Perhaps not,' he said. 'But, when it came down to it, you'd have fought. You're a survivor, Amanda. In fact, you were having second thoughts about jumping, even before I got to you.'

'That's not true,' she said shakily, replacing her cup on the table. 'I wanted to die. I still want to.'

'Simply because you found Nigel cavorting in bed with another lady?' He shook his head. 'I think you're made of stronger stuff than that, my child. I think, when you ran, you were hurt and confused and wanting, in some muddled way, to hit back at Nigel—to punish him—hurt him as he'd hurt you. I followed you, in the first instance, because I was worried about you driving in the state you were in. I thought you might crash the car.'

'I didn't see you.'

'I didn't intend you to,' he said equably. 'Would you like some more tea?'

She said an ungracious, 'No,' then added reluctantly, 'Thank you,' because she supposed he meant to be kind, although kindness wasn't a quality she'd particularly associated with him before.

But then, she didn't really know very much about him at all, except that he was Nigel's older brother, and the head of Templeton Laboratories. When she had first met him, she'd been conscious of a vague disappointment, because she supposed she'd been expecting an older edition of Nigel, with the same outgoing charm and rakish good looks.

But Malory Templeton had been totally different, shorter than Nigel—barely six feet, she estimated—and built on a more slender scale, too. Their basic colouring was the same, they were both brown-haired and blue-eyed, but Malory's skin was almost pale when contrasted with Nigel's robust tan.

He had been quietly polite, his handshake firm as he greeted her, but Amanda had found his manner chilling, and was absurdly glad that he and Nigel inhabited such very different worlds. He was almost like Nigel's shadow, she'd thought.

Now, at the worst moment of her life, their worlds seemed to have collided, and she felt uneasy about it.

She said abruptly, 'What were you doing at Calthorpe, anyway? You don't usually go to watch Nigel. You're not interested in rally-driving. He told me so.'

'I'm not,' he said briefly, and there was a silence. At last he said, 'I suppose I went there for a confrontation.' His mouth twisted slightly. 'You see, you're not the only injured party in all this.' His gaze met hers squarely. 'The lady with Nigel was someone I'd come to think of as mine.'

Amanda's lips parted in a soundless gasp, but she couldn't think of a single thing to say.

He added pleasantly, 'Or did you think the sole object of my affections was a test-tube?'

The blunt answer to that was 'probably', but she didn't give it. Yet, if she was honest, it was difficult to imagine anyone as colourless as Malory Templeton being involved in a passionate, full-blooded affair.

She said stiltedly, 'I'm sorry.'

'So am I,' he said. 'But at least I had the advantage of suspecting what was going on. I didn't just—walk in on it.' He paused. 'If I'd arrived there sooner, I might have been able to stop you.'

'But you wouldn't have been able to stop it happening,' she said in a low voice, staring at the flames flickering round the logs in the hearth.

'No,' he agreed, and there was another silence.

At last, curiosity impelled her to say, 'And what about you, Malory? Are you a survivor, too?'

He said drily, 'Well, I'm not leaving here to look for another flooded river. My pride may be damaged, but my heart's still intact. I hadn't got anywhere near the stage of offering it—or my hand.' He flicked a glance at Amanda's fingers. 'I note you're no longer wearing your ring.'

'I threw it at him,' she confessed. She had bruised her knuckle wrenching the solitaire off. The slight pain had seemed the only reality in an increasingly nightmare situation: Nigel's sex-flushed face turned unbelievingly towards the door, the glazed eyes focusing, his mouth gaping ridiculously, like a fish's. All that, she thought, would haunt her for ever. A faint flush rose in her cheeks. That, and the image of the naked girl straddling him so ecstatically.

Malory said, 'It would be far better not to think about it.' He looked at her expressionlessly, and her colour deepened. Was he some kind of clair-voyant? she wondered angrily. It was bad enough that he was here, intruding on her life at all—prying into her misery. She didn't want him trampling over her thoughts as well.

She said with faint defiance, 'You have a better idea?'

'I think you should change your skirt and stockings,' he said unexpectedly. 'The ones you're wearing are in rather a mess, and you don't want to look as if you've been through some kind of trauma when Nigel shows up.'

She gasped. 'You think he'll come here?'

'I'd put money on it,' he said laconically. 'He'll be coming to confess his fault and ask for absol-ution. But not,' he added, 'for penance.'

Amanda felt as if she was dreaming. She said, 'You can't be suggesting that I should overlook this—simply pretend it never happened and forgive him?'

'I'm suggesting nothing. Just telling you what Nigel will expect. My stepmother, you see, always forgave him everything, so he's grown up with the idea that none of his peccadilloes will ever be held against him.'

Amanda said hotly, 'Sleeping with his brother's girlfriend is hardly a—a whatever.'

'I don't think he'll agree with you. It isn't a serious relationship between them, you know. Just a little sexual romp, with some mutual guilt for added spice.' He glanced at his watch. 'I expected him some time ago, but no doubt he's still pre-paring his defence.'

'Defence?' Amanda repeated. 'What possible defence can there be?'

Malory considered for a moment. 'Well, the best form of defence is supposed to be attack, so in his shoes I'd probably opt for that. I'd claim that you'd driven me to infidelity through sheer sexual frustration.'

Amanda sat very upright, and stared at him. She said, 'How do you know that—I mean, that Nigel and I don't—that we haven't...' She broke off, flushing furiously.

'Because you have virginal eyes,' Malory said almost casually, adding, 'Quite a rarity these days.'

Amanda had always presumed he was as uninterested in her as she'd been in him. It was, therefore, disturbing to realise that, in fact, he'd been observing her so closely.

She took a breath. 'That's a—bloody chauvinist remark.'

'Yes, isn't it?' he said cordially. 'I'm not immune from the normal male responses, or faults, if you prefer.' He paused. 'You really think I'm a dull stick, don't you, Amanda? Well, compared to Nigel, I suppose I am. And apparently Clare thought so, too.'

The faint bitterness in his voice wasn't lost on her, penetrating momentarily her own unhappiness and resentment. But she didn't want to know about this more human side of him. She preferred him civil, but aloof and bloodless, the way she'd always thought of him.

Twenty-four hours ago, she hadn't known that Malory was involved even marginally with anyone.

Now, the picture of this Clare with her beautiful face and lush, full-breasted nakedness seemed indelibly printed on her mind. As, no doubt, it was on Malory's.

She got to her feet. 'Well, I'll go and change.'

He cast a slightly frowning glance at her legs. 'And put some antiseptic on those scratches while you're about it.'

She was tempted to salute smartly, but controlled herself. Instead, she was half astonished, half appalled to hear herself saying, with faint challenge, 'Anyway, they're not stockings. They're tights.'

She'd expected to embarrass him, to see him avert his gaze hurriedly. But, deliberately, he allowed his scrutiny to intensify, to linger where her still-damp skirt clung to her thighs.

'What a disappointment,' he drawled. The frown had vanished, and the challenge was being returned, she realised, with interest. 'Like most men, I much prefer stockings.'

She wanted to say, 'Another chauvinist response,' but she couldn't because she was the one who was embarrassed now, knowing that she would stumble over the words. Or, indeed, anything she attempted to say.

The most dignified, in fact, the only course seemed to be a silent retreat upstairs.

In her bedroom, she took a long look at herself in the mirror, and grimaced. She'd dressed so carefully for that surprise reunion with Nigel. Now, the straight cream skirt was stained with damp and streaked with lichen, and she'd scuffed the toes of her new shoes, too.

And her skin was dreadful, she thought with a pang: blotchy with weeping, her eyes red and puffy.

If Nigel was really on his way here, she didn't want to face him like this. In fact, she never wanted to see him again.

She stripped and put on her robe before crossing the narrow landing to the bathroom. She ran herself a warm bath, adding a capful of Savlon to the water before lowering herself into it.

In spite of the warmth, she found she was shivering. She supposed it was reaction to everything that had happened. She'd set out that day for Calthorpe, as nervous as a kitten, but burning with anticipation at the same time.

'Love me,' Nigel had pleaded hoarsely so many times. 'Trust me.'

And she'd been prepared to do just that, telling herself it was absurd to attach so much importance to the symbolism of a white wedding—a wedding night. She loved Nigel, she wanted to give herself to him, and her mother's departure for London, coupled with the few days' leave allotted to her by her grateful, vacation-bound boss, had seemed to provide the ideal opportunity for her to prove to Nigel, once and for all, that she desired him just as much as he seemed to want her.

He had finished third in the rally, one of his best results ever, and she had rung the hotel where he was staying to congratulate him the previous evening, so she knew his room number.

But the planned surprise had rebounded on her, she thought, wincing, as the pain of his betrayal lashed at her again. She had never loved anyone else but Nigel. And now she never would. Never could.

She had first met Nigel just over a year ago, when the company she worked for had been helping sponsor a rally in the Lake District, and had held a lavish reception for the drivers. Amanda had been roped in to help, making sure that everyone mixed socially, and that the drinks circulated too.

She didn't know what had made her look up at one point, but it had been to find Nigel watching her from the other side of the room. He had raised his glass in a silent and admiring toast, and she had turned away, blushing and biting her lip, wishing savagely that she had several more years' maturity and a wealth of sophistication to draw on.

When he had made his way to her side, she hadn't been able to believe it. He was already a name in rally circles—one of its young, rising stars, the papers said, although a few sports writers had commented in caustic terms on his good fortune in having the Templeton money to back up his ambitions.

Amanda had no illusions about herself. She was attractive enough, she supposed, if rather over-slender, with her green eyes, and a mane of reddish-chestnut hair which she kept tied back for work. But she had no wealthy background, nor any kind of star quality to compete with Nigel's.

But, miraculously, that seemed to be what he wanted. And when, after a few months of wining, dining and dancing together, he'd asked her to marry him, she'd agreed without hesitation, hardly able to credit her good luck. And she'd been living in a fool's paradise ever since, she reminded herself with angry bitterness.

She was brought out of her unhappy reverie with startling suddenness by an imperative rattling at the bathroom door.

Malory's voice said sternly, 'Are you in there, Amanda? What's taking so long?'

'I'm having a bath,' she called back, remembering too late that she'd forgotten to lock the door, and looking round frantically for the nearest towel.

Through the panels of the door, his voice sounded grim. 'As long as that's all. I'm counting to ten, Amanda, and if you're not out of there by then, I'm coming in.'

She realised he was concerned in case she was overdosing, or cutting her wrists with her own miniature razor, and a tiny bubble of hysteria welled up inside her.

But, meanwhile, the countdown seemed to be proceeding, and she hauled herself rapidly out of the cooling water, blotting the excess moisture from her body before tugging on her robe and knotting its sash firmly round her waist.

Malory had reached 'Two!' when she flung open the door and confronted him.

She said, 'I don't need a minder.' She sounded altogether more uptight than she'd intended and, as his brows rose, made haste to modify her approach. 'Malory, this afternoon I went slightly crazy. I don't quite know what happened, but I do know that it's not going to happen again.'

'So will I please go and leave you to your own devices,' he finished for her.

Amanda flushed. 'Well—yes.'

He studied her for a moment, his face expressionless. Then he said, 'Just as you wish,' and, turning, went downstairs. She was brushing her hair in the bedroom when she heard his car drive away, and drew a breath of profound relief.

She couldn't deny that he'd been very kind, but it irked her that it should ever have been necessary. She had behaved like the top hysterical idiot of all time, and that was quite bad enough, without having Malory Templeton observing the whole performance as if she was some specimen for dissection.

Of course, he'd had an emotional set-back of his own, although he'd seemed to take it pretty much in his stride. Amanda put down her brush. If she was honest, she decided, she couldn't altogether blame Clare for chasing Nigel. He had a glamour that Malory totally lacked. Malory might be rich, and be the brains behind Templeton Laboratories, but in other ways he was pretty much of a nonentity. In fact, she found it difficult to recall exactly what he looked like. But what did that matter, she asked herself impatiently, when almost certainly she would never be obliged to see him again?

Nigel arrived an hour later. Amanda hadn't heard his car, but the two imperative rings at the doorbell were his trademark and, reluctantly, she went to answer his summons.

Face and voice subdued, he said, 'Hello, darling. Are you going to let me in?'

She stood silently aside to admit him to the hall.

His blue eyes surveyed her wryly, then he said, 'Well, say it, love. Scream at me, hit me, tell me what a bastard I am. You're perfectly justified to call me anything you want.'

Amanda was thankful to hear her own voice so steady. 'What's the point of calling you names? It won't change a thing. I don't know why you've come here, Nigel, but . . .'

'Isn't it obvious?' he interrupted passionately. 'I'm here because I love you, Manda. Oh, I know that must be hard for you to credit, after what you saw today, but it's true all the same. This—Clare—doesn't mean a thing to me. We had a few drinks last night—and everything snowballed.'

'What was she doing there in the first place?' Amanda asked quietly.

'At Calthorpe?' He shrugged. 'Search me, love. Watching the closing stages of the rally, I suppose.'

She said, 'But she was Malory's girl, wasn't she?'

Something flickered in his eyes, then he shrugged again. 'They may have been seeing each other—who knows? Mal's private life is a closed book to me, and I doubt whether he opens it very much himself, either. After all, he's hardly a turn-on for any woman, in bed or out of it.'

The casual cruelty of it made her wince in swift distaste.

'You shouldn't say things like that about your own brother.'

'Half-brother,' he corrected, and she remembered picking Malory up on the same point—a lifetime ago, it seemed now. 'But we're not here to discuss Mal's sexual proclivities, if he has any.'

'Then why are we here?' Amanda asked wearily.

'To talk out this stupid mess, then put it behind us for ever,' he said intensely. 'For God's sake, Manda, we have too much going for us to allow one idiotic slip on my part to come between us. After all, it's you I want to marry, not some silly little slag.'

She heard herself say, 'It's not as simple as that . . .' and heard yet another echo from her conversation with Malory.

'But it is, or it could be if you'd let it.' Nigel took a step towards her, his face darkening a little as she backed away. For a moment, a sharp tension enwrapped them both, then he relaxed deliberately, giving vent to a little sigh.

'So, what do you want me to do?' he demanded resignedly. 'Plead with you? Grovel? Go on my knees? I will, if that's what it takes. But just remember, Mandy, all this would never have happened if you'd been less of the icy little virgin.'

She'd been warned to expect this, but it was still a shock to hear the words on his lips.

She said, 'Are you saying it's my fault that you couldn't stay faithful—even for a few weeks?'

'It's nothing to do with faithfulness, as such,' he dismissed impatiently. 'I just happen to have a very high sex-drive, and this look-but-don't-touch thing of yours has been driving me up the wall. If I'd

had you, darling, all the Clares in the world couldn't
have lured me away. Can't you understand that?'

'And if you'd really loved me as I thought, then
it couldn't have happened, either,' Amanda said
tiredly. 'I don't think we're even talking about the
same things. I'm sorry, Nigel, but I've stopped
trusting you, and I can't marry a man I can't trust.'

He said, 'Darling, you can't mean that. I've
apologised. What more can I do?'

'There's nothing.' Tears were threatening again,
and she lifted her chin. 'I'd just like you to leave,
please.'

Nigel was staring at her, as if he could not believe his ears. When he spoke, his voice sounded
hoarse. 'Now, listen, you little bitch! You're not
throwing me over like this. I'll...' He stopped
abruptly as the kitchen door swung open with a
small creak, and Malory walked into the hall.

He said dispassionately, 'I think for once in your
life you're going to have to take "no" for an
answer, Nigel. Why don't you go?'

Nigel's eyes narrowed as he looked from one to
the other. 'Well, this is all very cosy,' he said tightly.
He turned a glittering look on Amanda. 'No
wonder you were so well informed about the lovely
Clare, darling. So, old Mal came whingeing to you,
did he? I wondered why you'd just happened to
turn up at precisely the wrong moment today.'

She was about to protest that he was wrong, that
it hadn't been like that, but realised in time that
the truth might lead to explanations about the real
reason behind her trip to Calthorpe that she would
much rather keep secret, and her courage failed her.

She said, 'That doesn't matter now. Nothing matters. Just go—please.'

'Leaving you to weep on each other's shoulders? How very touching,' Nigel said mockingly. 'Like two ice-cubes meeting in a fridge. My God, you two could be the pairing of the century—the Virgin and the Stuffed Shirt!' He sent them both a blazing look, then turned on his heel and strode to the front door. The whole cottage seemed to shake as he slammed it.

Amanda thought, I'll remember this moment until the day I die.

She felt the pain uncurling, beginning to tear at her again, and heard Malory say gently, 'Are you all right?'

Proudly, she raised her head. 'Yes,' she said.

CHAPTER TWO

AMANDA said, 'Why did you come back?'

'In actual fact, I never went away.'

They sat facing each other across the kitchen table.

Malory went on, 'I simply drove my car round to the back lane, and walked up through the kitchen garden.'

Amanda said stonily, 'I asked you to leave. I thought you *had* left.'

He gave her a weary look. 'Yes, I know, and you don't need a minder, and you're no longer suicidal. But that wasn't all of it. I'd gathered you intended to give Nigel his marching orders, and I wasn't sure how he'd take that. I wanted to make certain there was no—rough stuff.'

Colour rose hotly in Amanda's face. 'That's an abominable insinuation to make!'

'Then I withdraw it unreservedly,' he said calmly. 'Nigel would have taken your dismissal on the chin, and left like a lamb without my unwarranted intervention.' He paused. 'Wouldn't he?'

Amanda bit her lip and didn't reply. At last, she said curtly, 'Hardly very dignified, skulking in someone's kitchen. Supposing I'd come in and found you?'

He shrugged. 'We'd be having this conversation then, rather than now.'

'You think you have an answer for everything, don't you?' she said crossly.

He shook his head. 'On the contrary. But I have had the advantage of knowing Nigel for the past twenty-six years, which gives me an insight into the way he's likely to respond to any given situation.' Another pause. 'Which is why I don't think you should be alone tonight.'

'My God!' Amanda's brows lifted contemptuously. 'You really believe in putting the boot in, don't you? What do you imagine he'll do? Come back and rape me?'

'I didn't say that.'

'And if I say I don't want you here?' she bit back at him. 'What then? After all, I hardly know you. For all I know, you might be planning to rape me yourself.'

'How very true,' he said. 'What a fascinating night it promises to be.' There was an icy distaste in his voice which got to her.

She mumbled, 'I'm sorry. That was—a stupid thing to say. I'm still not thinking very clearly.' She made herself meet his gaze. 'But I can't honestly put you to any more trouble. I—I'm sure you mean well...' She stopped again. 'Oh, God, that sounds even worse. What I'm trying to say is, you must have plans of your own for this evening, and I'll be all right—really.' It sounded lame, and she knew it, but she wasn't even convinced herself. She was tense and on edge, emotionally vulnerable. The last thing she needed, or wanted, was to be alone.

She found herself saying reluctantly, 'Although there is the spare bedroom...'

'Then it's settled.' His tone was matter of fact, without a trace of smugness. 'Now, let's get down to practicalities. Did you leave your keys in the car, or were you planning to jump with them?'

She gaped at him for a moment. 'Oh—they're still in the ignition.'

He nodded. 'Then I'd better walk down to the bridge and bring the car back, before someone takes a fancy to it. Shall I put it away for you in the garage?'

It had to be one of the most bizarre conversations she'd ever taken part in! She wondered crazily what he'd have done with the damned car if she had really jumped, then pulled herself together.

'Er—yes, please.' She paused. 'And I'll make a meal for us.' Nigel had always been incredibly fussy about food, requiring even a simple steak to be cooked to the exact minute he specified. Perhaps it was a family trait. 'Have you any particular likes or dislikes?'

He said politely, 'I don't think so. Whatever's going will be fine.'

Neutral could well be his middle name, Amanda thought crossly when he'd gone.

Her mother invariably left the refrigerator stocked as if for a siege, and Amanda extracted some lamb chops and the ingredients for a salad, before scrubbing two large potatoes, wrapping them in foil, and putting them in the Aga to bake.

She wondered whether Malory would expect to be entertained formally in the dining-room, and decided to pre-empt the issue by laying the kitchen table.

She still wasn't sure why he was staying, or why she was allowing it, but she had a feeling it was going to be a long, awkward evening. Perhaps a drink might ease the situation, Amanda thought, although he'd probably opt for a small, dry sherry. She decided she'd better go along to the drawing-room, and see what there was. As she went through the hall, the telephone rang.

Her heart sank. Mother, she thought. Somehow, she was going to have to break the news that all the wedding arrangements undertaken so far were going to have to be cancelled. She only hoped Mrs Conroy hadn't bought her outfit yet.

Sighing, she lifted the receiver and gave the number. But, instead of the excited rush of feminine chatter she'd expected, she found herself greeted by a profound silence. Puzzled, she gave the number again, and jiggled the rest. But the silence continued.

She said rather doubtfully, 'Hello—can you hear me?' Still nothing. But it wasn't a dead silence, she realised. It was very much alive, because she could hear the faint sound of breathing at the other end.

Amanda's nose wrinkled, and she slammed the receiver back on the rest, just as Malory walked back through the front door. He gave her a surprised look.

'Is something the matter?'

'Not really,' she said tautly. 'Just a crank phone call.' She managed a smile. 'And all in silence, too. I didn't even manage to learn any useful obscenities.'

He glanced at the phone, his brows drawing together in a swift frown. 'Well, I know a fair number. You'd better let me answer next time.'

'Oh, there won't be a next time.' Amanda tried to sound breezy. 'Once they realise you're not going to flip, they try someone else.'

'You've experienced this type of thing before?'

'Loads of times,' she lied. 'Would you like a drink?'

Malory shrugged off his overcoat. 'Thanks, I'll have a large whisky.' He gave her an enquiring glance. 'Have I said something funny?'

'Oh, no.' Amanda swallowed. 'You're just—rather unexpected sometimes.'

'Having always believed I was all too predictable, I'll take that as a compliment.' The phone rang again, and he reached for it, saying curtly, 'Hello?'

If that's Mother, she'll have a heart attack, Amanda thought faintly. But she could hear no outraged squeaks. She looked at Malory, her eyes mutely enquiring, and he nodded. He was leaning against the hall table, looking very relaxed, a thumb hooked into the belt of his trousers. And he continued to stand there as minute after minute ticked past.

At last he said smoothly into the mouthpiece, 'I'm prepared to stand here all night, if that's what you want.' He replaced the receiver with a slight grimace. 'Our caller rang off,' he said. 'I think only one can play this particular game.' He gave Amanda a long look. 'Well?'

She bit her lip. 'It's a crank, I tell you.'

Malory shrugged. 'Anything you say. Now, how about that drink?'

He followed her into the drawing-room, and watched as she poured a generous measure into a crystal tumbler, adding a splash of soda at his direction.

She said passionately, 'It isn't Nigel. It isn't!'

He lifted his glass to her with an ironic glance. 'Here's to loyalty, however misplaced.'

She said, her voice shaking, 'You really hate him, don't you?'

He considered that for a moment or two, then said, 'No.'

'Then why are you so down on him—imagining that he would do anything as childish as those phone calls?'

'Because it's the kind of mischief he used to revel in,' Malory said, after another pause.

'In the past, maybe.' Amanda shrugged that away. 'But you haven't lived under the same roof with Nigel for a long time now. He's changed. He's grown up. Can't you understand that?'

'There was certainly room for some maturity,' Malory agreed caustically, 'but his recent behaviour doesn't show much evidence of it.'

It was infuriating not to be able to contradict him flatly, and Amanda seethed in silence.

Finally she said, 'Are you sure you're not just jealous—because the lady you wanted preferred Nigel?'

'Oh, I'm jealous all right.' He was smiling faintly as he said it, but Amanda felt a small frisson of something like fear shiver its way down her spine.

'In fact, I don't think I shall ever forgive him for it.'

She felt as if the cool, civilised mask had slipped for a moment, and it disturbed her. He had definitely cared for Clare more than she'd realised, she decided, and was brought, reeling, back to the conventional world by his polite, 'Do you mind if I switch on the television?'

She said hastily, 'Do—please,' and beat a retreat back to the kitchen.

It was becoming evident that Malory Templeton was something of an enigma, she realised as she made the vinaigrette dressing for the salad. She had never thought Nigel and his half-brother were over-fond of each other, but now it seemed her erstwhile fiancé had made himself a real enemy.

'This is a charming house,' Malory commented later as they ate the blackberry ice-cream Amanda had produced from the freezer for dessert. 'Do you live here all the time?'

She shook her head. 'Mostly, I live in London. I share a flat with three other girls.' She smiled faintly. 'But I come down here every chance I get.'

'I'm not surprised. Has your mother been alone for some time?'

'Yes, Daddy died four years ago of a heart attack. It was—very sudden.'

'They often are,' he said. 'My father died of the same thing, but in his case he had a number of advance warnings—all of which he chose to ignore.' He sounded rueful.

'Do you miss him?'

'Yes, I do,' he admitted. 'We weren't very close when I was a child, but we became friends as I got older.' He paused. 'Particularly after my stepmother disappeared from the scene.'

'You didn't like her?'

'When she married my father I was prepared to worship her.' He shook his head. 'She was quite the most beautiful thing I'd ever seen in my life. But it didn't take long to discover that she didn't want my adoration, or any other part of me. However, I even forgave her that when she had Nigel. I'd always wanted a younger brother.'

'Then it's a pity you haven't—a closer relationship now,' she said stiltedly.

'There was never really an opportunity,' he said. 'Camilla had decided in advance I was going to be jealous of her baby, and would probably try to harm him in some way, so every attempt I made to approach him was regarded with the gravest suspicion. I was shunted away to school as soon as was decently possible, and Nigel didn't even follow me there. We grew up like parallel lines—close but never meeting. By the time we did get to know one another, it was to discover how very little we had in common.'

'That's a pity.'

He shrugged. 'That's the way it goes.' He looked at her. 'You're an only child?'

She nodded. 'Didn't Nigel tell you?'

'He actually told me very little about you, except that you were engaged, accompanied by a reluctant invitation to meet you and your mother.'

Amanda smiled wryly. 'That was a rather heavy evening. I had the feeling you didn't altogether approve of me.'

'That would have been very presumptuous of me.' He added, after a pause, 'I think I was merely amazed that Nigel had decided to settle down. Also, we'd had a row on the way here. Nigel is due to inherit some shares in the company on his marriage, and he wanted to push matters forward. I had to tell him it couldn't be done, and he wasn't very pleased. He thought I should have bent the rules in his favour.'

'Could you have done so?' she asked gravely.

He said, 'No,' and there was a silence. Then he said. 'May I help with the washing up?'

'There isn't any. I simply load the dishwasher.' Amanda got up. 'And, as it's rather ancient and temperamental, it prefers a hand it knows.'

'Then I'll make the coffee,' he said promptly. He had beautiful teeth when he smiled, she noticed. 'Don't look so stunned, Amanda. I'm reasonably house-trained. If you'll show me where the sheets and blankets are kept, I'll even make up my own bed.'

'It's already done,' she began, and paused as the phone began to ring again.

'Load the dishwasher,' Malory said. 'I'll answer it.'

Amanda found that her hands were trembling as she scraped the dishes and put them into the machine.

'Wrong number,' Malory said briefly when he returned, but she didn't believe him.

They drank their coffee in the drawing-room, watching a re-run of *The French Connection*. Watching Malory covertly, Amanda decided that the violence of the New York drugs scene must be as far removed from his environment as it was possible to get.

'He's got a bijou residence where he's waited on hand and foot by devoted retainers,' Nigel had told her once, derisively. 'And when he's not at the labs trying to produce a wonder-drug that will cure every known disease, he's in his box at the opera. Coming into contact with the real world must be a hell of a shock to his system. Fortunately for him, he doesn't have to do it very often.'

But today's events had been the real world with a vengeance, Amanda thought with a little sigh, which she hastily converted into a yawn as he looked at her.

'You're tired?'

'I think I must be.' It wasn't strictly the truth, but she was eager to go upstairs and shut her door. The evening had turned into a rather unnerving experience, and it wasn't altogether due to the crank calls. Sharing this kind of intimacy with Malory was—strange, and she would be glad when it was over.

She had tried phoning her mother earlier, but there was no reply, and she guessed that she and Elaine had gone to the theatre. I'll have to get through to her in the morning, she thought.

And then, slowly and painfully, she would try to get her life back on to an even keel again—learning to live without Nigel.

She yawned ostentatiously, and got to her feet. 'Well—goodnight. I hope you have everything you need.' She tried a smile. 'I'm sorry I can't provide pyjamas.'

'That's no sacrifice. I never wear them.' He had risen, too, and was walking over to her. Amanda had kicked off her shoes as she often did, and she felt oddly dwarfed suddenly.

He said quietly, 'Goodnight, Amanda, sleep well.' And for one brief, troubled moment, she thought he was going to kiss her, and her whole body went into shock at the idea.

She found she was backing away, babbling something incoherent about the spark-guard for the fire, and fled.

She was still awake an hour later when he came upstairs to bed, but he passed her door without hesitating, and she lay in the darkness, castigating herself for having behaved like an idiot in front of him, yet again.

She was just asking herself for the umpteenth time where the harm would have been in a brief, farewell peck on the cheek, and still receiving no satisfactory answer, when she fell asleep.

The crash seemed to shatter the room. For one ter-rified, screaming moment, Amanda thought the cottage had been bombed, then she made herself reach for the switch of the bedside lamp, realising as she did so that a strong current of cold air was reaching her from somewhere.

As the lamp came on, she cried out. There was a gaping hole in the middle of her window-pane, and a half-brick lay on the carpet, surrounded by shards of broken glass. There were even some splinters on her duvet, she realised, shuddering.

Her door opened, and Malory put his head, and one bare, surprisingly muscular, shoulder into the room.

'What the hell was that?' he demanded, then stopped. 'Christ!'

'Don't come in.' Amanda's voice shook. 'There's glass everywhere.'

'I've no intention of coming in until I've put something on,' he said curtly. 'In the meantime, stay exactly where you are.'

He was back, it seemed, within seconds, still fastening his zip as he came into the room.

Amanda said with a little sob, 'It must be vandals.'

'Of course.' His voice was heavily ironic. 'There are always hordes of them at this time of year.' He looked around him. 'Where are your slippers?'

'With your pyjamas.'

His mouth tightened. 'Then it seems I'll have to provide transport.' As he approached the bed, Amanda could hear glass scrunching under his feet. He leaned down and pulled back the duvet. 'Put your arms round my neck, and I'll carry you,' he directed.

'Carry me where?' Amanda made an unavailing snatch at the duvet, thankful that her nightgown had been bought for cosiness rather than glamour.

'To the room I'm using,' he said, rather too patiently.

She swallowed. 'But where will you go?'

'I'll clear up the glass and fasten something over that window, then spend what remains of the night in here.' He paused. 'Or have you some objection?'

She said, 'Aren't you going to see if you can find—whoever did this?'

His mouth twisted. '"Whoever" is probably in a car, and well away by this time. I'm not embarking on any wild-goose chase at this hour of the morning. Now, shall we make a start?' He bent towards her and, reluctantly, Amanda allowed herself to be lifted out of bed and into his arms.

He wasn't anywhere near as effete as she'd thought, she discovered with amazement. He'd picked her up without the slightest effort, and she could feel the play of his muscles under her hand as she steadied herself.

On the landing, she said, 'There isn't any glass here, so you can put me down,' and he obeyed so promptly it was almost an insult.

He said prosaically, 'Where will I find a dustpan and brush?'

'In the kitchen cupboard, next to the back door.' She moistened her dry lips with the tip of her tongue. 'And there are some cardboard boxes, too, that you might be able to use to cover the window.' She put a hand to her head. 'Oh, this is all crazy! None of it can be happening.'

'Of course it isn't.' Malory gave her a gentle push in the direction of the spare room. 'Now, go and get some rest and tell yourself in the morning that it's all been a bad dream.'

But she couldn't relax. Lying in the warm hollow his body had created, Amanda listened tensely to the sounds of movement along the passage. When they eventually ceased, she called to him.

'What's the matter?' He came to stand in the doorway.

'I'm frightened.' Her teeth were chattering, but not because she was cold. 'Do you think he—they will come back?'

If he'd noticed that revealing self-correction, he made no comment. 'I don't think so. I imagine the purpose of the exercise—to give you a good fright— has been achieved.'

She stared at him. 'You really do think it's Nigel, don't you?'

'Yes.' His voice was matter of fact.

'It can't be!' she denied vehemently. 'No grown man could be so—childish.'

He smiled. 'I don't think you can have known a great many grown men,' he said with a touch of cynicism. 'But perhaps we could continue this debate in the morning. I'd like to get some sleep.'

A voice she hardly recognised as hers said, 'I don't want to be on my own. Stay with me— please?' She saw the blank incredulity in his face and began to stammer, 'I—I don't mean . . .'

He said rather drily, 'I'm sure you don't.' He hesitated. 'Very well, Amanda. I should have re-alised that appointing myself your guardian would have its drawbacks.' He walked over to the bed. 'At the same time, I hope you don't think I plan to spend the rest of the night in that chair or on the floor.' He kicked off his shoes, and lay down beside her, on top of the quilt. 'This seems a suitably chaste arrangement under the circumstances.'

She ventured, 'But won't you be rather cold? You can use the duvet, if you want.'

He said evenly, 'No, thank you. Don't push your luck, Amanda. In spite of anything Nigel may have told you, I am not a eunuch.' He reached out and switched off the lamp. 'Now, go to sleep.'

Face burning, she mumbled, 'Goodnight.'

She must be completely insane, she thought, asking Malory to share a bed with her like this, but the prospect of lying alone in the darkness, waiting for the next unnerving incident, was more than she could bear. She hadn't really stopped to consider Malory's feelings or reactions at all.

Yet she couldn't deny the reassurance of the weight of his body beside her on the bed, and the steadiness of his breathing. She didn't feel she deserved this kindness from him, but it seemed to be there for her, just the same.

With a little sigh, she closed her eyes, and within a few minutes, against all her expectations, was fast asleep.

She awoke slowly the next morning to the aroma of frying bacon, and lay for a few minutes staring at her unfamiliar surroundings, wondering confusedly why she wasn't in her own room. Then remembrance flooded back, and she shot out of bed and down the passage to her doorway.

The square of cardboard over the broken window was like some grim exclamation mark, she thought, as she trod with care to the wardrobe and extracted jeans and a sweater. She washed and dressed swiftly, and ran downstairs.

Malory was seated at the kitchen table. The smile he sent her was polite, but guarded. 'I was just coming to wake you,' he said. 'Your breakfast is keeping warm.'

Blushing a little, she brought her plate to the table and sat down opposite him. 'You shouldn't wait on me.' She added self-consciously, 'I—I went out like a light, last night.'

'So I noticed.' He glanced at his watch. 'I really should be going. Is there someone in the village who can fix that window for you?'

'Mr Ambrose does all the jobs like that. I'll phone him presently.' She smiled awkwardly. 'You seem to have got rid of the broken glass.'

'I used the vacuum first thing, while you were still giving your Sleeping Beauty performance.'

'Oh.' Amanda swallowed. 'You did that? Well, it makes me feel worse than ever—about everything.'

'Entirely unnecessary,' he said calmly. 'Last night, you needed a friend. Well, you've got one.' He held out a hand to her. 'Agreed?'

She allowed his fingers to close round hers. 'Agreed.' She hesitated. 'I'm sorry I've been such a fool.'

'You're probably entitled to be.' He gave her a searching look. 'Will you be all right alone today, or is there someone who could stay with you?'

'I'll be fine,' she said brightly. 'And my mother will be returning later.'

'Excellent.' He got to his feet. 'Goodbye, then.'

And this time, Amanda discovered, he really had left. When she checked, trying to be casual about it, a little while later, his car had vanished. And so, apparently, had he—on a permanent basis.

She wandered back into the cottage and shut the door. In spite of his remark about being her friend, she never expected to see Malory again. She wasn't sure she even wanted to.

He must think she was a complete nutcase, she told herself, and, what was worse, something of a tease as well.

Stay with me—please, she mimicked herself savagely. God, what must he have thought? She was lucky he hadn't even made a token pass. And it wasn't very flattering to his masculinity that she hadn't really considered such an eventuality when she'd made her plea. She'd only been thinking in terms of companionship and comfort.

Perhaps, in spite of his rather edged remark, he didn't have a very high sex-drive, she thought, shrugging. It occurred to her with an ache of her heart that Nigel would have made more than the most of such an opportunity.

No, Malory was a mystery all right, and she had enough confusion in her life already, without embarking on the pointless exercise of trying to figure out what made him tick.

Ships that pass in the night, she told herself resolutely as she headed to the phone to call Mr Ambrose. And better that she and Malory Templeton remain that way. Far better.

CHAPTER THREE

WHEN she heard the sound of a car outside two hours later, Amanda found she was mentally nerving herself to meet her mother's reproaches. Mrs Conroy had been almost distraught when Amanda phoned her with the bald statement that her engagement was over.

'Darling, you can't be serious!' she had wailed. 'You've had some silly tiff, that's all. I know it is. I'm coming home immediately to talk to you.'

She had rung off before Amanda could tell her that the time for talking was long past. But then, her mother adored Nigel, and probably wouldn't have listened.

Amanda put down the crossword puzzle she'd been staring at as if the clues were in Sanskrit, and went into the hall to meet her mother, trying to think of some placatory remark as she did so.

When the doorbell rang, she felt almost reprieved. It must be Mr Ambrose, she thought with relief. He'd promised in response to her urgency to 'pop along as soon as maybe' and see to her bedroom window. With luck, it might even be repaired before Mrs Conroy returned, and her mother need know nothing about it.

The last person she expected to see on the doorstep was Nigel.

If she'd had her wits about her, she would have slammed the door in his face, but, as she stood, gaping at him, he walked past her into the hall. He was rather pale, and there was a small muscle jumping at the corner of his mouth. He stood flicking his driving gloves against the palm of his hand.

He said, 'Manda, I had to come here. I couldn't keep away. We've both had time to think—to calm down. You've got to listen to me.' He looked round. 'Are you alone this time?' The question was edged. He was asking if Malory had gone, she knew, yet she felt curiously reluctant to tell him she was alone in the house.

She lifted her chin. 'I have someone fixing the bedroom window.'

'Oh?' His surprise was too elaborate. 'Is it broken?'

She said thickly, 'You know it is, because you did it. What with that and those phone calls, you really surpassed yourself last night.'

He looked away, flushing. 'I know—I know,' he said heavily. 'I think I must have gone slightly crazy. That's one of the reasons I came here—to ask you to forgive me for all that rubbish.'

'A brick through the window is hardly rubbish,' she said angrily. 'I could have been killed.'

'I told you, I wasn't thinking straight.' He took a step towards her. 'Darling, can't we sit down and talk our problems out, quietly and sensibly?'

'No, we can't. I thought I'd made that clear already.' Amanda stood her ground. 'There's nothing to discuss, Nigel. It's finished between us—over for good.'

'But when you said it you were too angry to listen to reason,' he said.

'Reason?' she echoed. 'Nigel, I caught you making love to someone else—to your brother's woman. What reason can there possibly be for that? What excuse?'

'That's what I'm here to explain.' He spread his hands in appeal. 'Manda, you have to let me defend myself. You can't just—condemn me like this. We still love each other—you know that, darling.'

'You have a very strange way of showing it,' Amanda countered coldly. 'But say what you have to say—if you must.'

He was silent for a moment. 'You don't have to tell me I've been a crass, insensitive fool. I know that. Since I met you, I always considered I was immune to temptation from other women. But it always existed.' His mouth twisted in self-deprecation. 'Rally-drivers have their groupies, too.'

'But I can't believe Clare was one of them.'

'No,' he conceded. 'But she made all the running, once she realised who I was. She kept phoning me—throwing herself at me.'

'So, she didn't just happen to be at Calthorpe?'

'No, she followed me there deliberately. I—I lied about that. She wouldn't let me alone. She kept pestering me.'

'Poor Nigel,' Amanda said with irony. 'How very trying for you. And, I suppose, in the end temptation just became too much. Or did she rape you?'

Dull colour rose in his face. 'No, of course not. But I'm no saint, sweetheart. I have my weaknesses, and maybe it's better for you to know about them before rather than after we're married.' As her lips parted in protest, he lifted his hand to halt whatever she was going to say. He said intensely, 'Because you are going to marry me, darling. You must. You're not going to let one stupid, spoiled little tart ruin our lives.' As he said it, he smiled at her, the blue eyes suddenly ingenuous and appealing. 'I need you, Manda.'

His hands reached for her, and she stepped back, away from him.

She said, 'You talk as if your—fling with Clare were the only issue involved, but it isn't. It's the way you've acted since. Those beastly phone calls—my window.'

'Darling.' Nigel was still smiling. 'I was beside myself—coming here and finding Malory with you was an awful jolt. I hung around for hours, waiting for him to leave.' He shook his head. 'When I realised he wasn't leaving, I went a bit mad, thinking all kinds of crazy things.' He laughed. 'I had this image of him in bed with you—up in that room. Somehow, I convinced myself that it was true, that it was happening, and something—snapped.' He gave a self-deprecatory sigh. 'Guilty conscience, I suppose, but I had this idea he was spending the night with you to get his own back over Clare. As if a sexless nonentity like Malory could ever dream up such a scheme!' He held out his hand to her. 'And as if you'd let him, anyway. After all, if I couldn't get near you, it's hardly likely you'd sleep with Mal.'

There was a long silence. Amanda could feel a slow, hot blush reaching up from her toes.

'Well, say something, darling.' Nigel sounded half amused, half impatient. 'Don't just stand there, or I shall start to think you let my dear brother into bed with you last night, after all.' And, as Amanda lifted her hands and pressed them to her burning face, he said slowly, his voice sinking to a whisper, 'Christ—it's true, isn't it? You slept with him, didn't you, you bitch?'

Sheer embarrassment, as well as anger, lit the fuse of Amanda's temper. 'Yes, I did.' She flung her head back defiantly. 'And I don't care if it was just vengeance for Clare.'

As soon as the words were out she regretted them, but it was too late. She couldn't go back and explain the truth about her night with Malory, because it would only expose them both to Nigel's scorn, and Malory didn't deserve that.

Nigel said hoarsely. 'You little whore! I wish that brick had killed you both.'

'I get the general idea.' Her voice shook. 'Now, get out of here, and don't come back.'

He half turned, then swung back towards her, his eyes raking her with a kind of furious greed. 'No—why should I? Now that Malory's given you one, you haven't got the excuse of your everlasting virginity to hold me off any more.' He laughed savagely. 'Maybe I should even be grateful to him for—opening the way for me, so to speak.'

His crudity made her cringe. She took another step backwards. 'Don't come near me.'

'You should have said that last night,' he jeered. 'You and Malory—my God! I didn't think it was possible. Does he have a chemical formula for sex, too? He's probably writing up the results of the experiment in triplicate at this very moment.'

'Don't you dare say things like that about Malory!' Amanda threw back at him fiercely. 'He has all the qualities you so signally lack—kindness and compassion, among them.'

'Oh, is that what you look for in a bed-partner?' His tone dripped contempt. 'My mistake, sweetheart. What did he do as foreplay—cry on your shoulder?'

'You're despicable...'

'And Malory, of course, is Sir Galahad,' Nigel almost snarled. 'If he's such a paragon, my sweet, why don't you marry him, instead?'

She said recklessly, 'I intend to...' and stopped with a little gasp as she saw Nigel's face darken with more than anger.

'That,' he said, too evenly, 'is if he still wants you, when I've finished with you.'

She'd retreated as far as the kitchen door, her hand clumsily, desperately fumbling with the handle, when she heard the back door open, and Mr Ambrose's stolid, dependable tones call, 'Miss Conroy—are you there, love? I've come to see to that little matter you mentioned.'

Her voice cracking, she called back, 'I'm here—in the hall.'

The door behind her opened, and Mr Ambrose stood there, looking at them, red-faced and sturdy, with shrewd eyes under bushy eyebrows. He said, 'Not butting in, am I?'

'No,' Amanda said breathlessly. 'Mr Templeton was just leaving—weren't you, Nigel?'

For one shocked moment, she thought he was going to hit her. Then he said, 'Yes, I'm going. But you'll be sorry for this, Amanda. I promise you that.'

As the front door closed behind him, she felt her legs begin to shake under her.

Mr Ambrose said, 'Seems in a bit of a state, your young man.' He paused, then added expressionlessly, 'A window, was it?'

She flushed. 'Yes.'

He had almost finished replacing the pane when Mrs Conroy arrived back. She was laden with parcels which she dumped on the drawing-room sofa before turning her gaze on Amanda.

'My dear child, you look positively dreadful. You're fretting for Nigel, I know you are. So why don't you go and phone him, and tell him you're sorry for whatever it was, and then we can all be happy again?'

Amanda said quietly, 'What makes you think I'm the one who should apologise?'

Mrs Conroy shrugged. 'Darling, what does it matter? It just needs one of you to make the first move.'

'The question's academic, anyway,' Amanda said. 'Nigel's been here already, and I sent him away.'

'Are you out of your mind?' her mother almost shrieked.

'I don't think so—not any more.'

'But what in the world could you have quarrelled about so drastically?' Mrs Conroy wailed. 'You were so well-suited—so perfect for each other in every way. And Nigel adored you.'

And flattered *you*, Amanda thought suddenly, but didn't say it.

She sat staring at the carpet while her mother continued her diatribe, naming Nigel's manifold perfections and desirability as a son-in-law.

She wished she could tell her the whole story, but it was impossible. The first thing her mother would want to know would be why she'd gone to Calthorpe in the first place. And that was un-answerable. One of the cornerstones of Mrs Conroy's philosophy was that unmarried people did not sleep together. The permissive society had only served to strengthen this firmly held belief, although Amanda suspected with wry affection that, as far as her mother was concerned, sex, even for married people, was not a major priority.

A broken engagement was enough of a disappointment for her mother to cope with. Mrs Conroy didn't need to know that her only child had been about to kick over the traces so shamelessly.

Suddenly Mrs Conroy paused, and stared up at the ceiling. 'There's someone moving around upstairs.'

'Only Mr Ambrose. He's mending a broken window in my room.'

Mrs Conroy's eyes widened. 'How on earth...?'

'I was doing some cleaning, and I had a slight accident, that's all.' Somehow, her mother had to be protected from the truth here, too.

'Oh, I don't understand any of this.' Her mother looked on the verge of tears. 'You seem determined to smash everything about you,' she added unfairly. 'And you don't even consider the work you're giving me. All kinds of arrangements will have to be cancelled—I only hope they haven't actually started printing the invitations. It's all too bad.'

Amanda touched her shoulder. 'Why don't you put your feet up, and let me make you some tea?' she urged gently. 'I'm sorry you've taken it like this, but you've got to believe that I can't be happy with Nigel. And I'd really rather not talk about it any more.'

It was a miserable weekend. Mrs Conroy kept her verbal reproaches to herself, but the long-suffering looks and sighs she sent in Amanda's direction were almost worse than a direct onslaught.

Amanda went for a long walk, and on Saturday afternoon occupied herself with some furious digging in the garden, using her inevitable weariness as an excuse for an early night.

She awoke on Sunday morning to the drowsy reflection that she only had a few more hours of silent recrimination to endure before she could go back to London and lose herself in her job. She wondered sleepily what her flatmates would have to say about her broken engagement and decided that, although Fiona and Maggie would treat it as a nine-day wonder, Jane wouldn't be altogether surprised.

She was shocked out of her somnolence by her mother's thin, wavering scream from downstairs.

What's Nigel done now? was Amanda's first thought as she threw back the bedclothes. Probably a dead cat through the letter-box!

But the hall seemed mercifully free of felines, alive or dead, as she arrived downstairs, tightening the sash of her robe. Mrs Conroy seemed to be confronted by nothing more startling than the Sunday papers.

'What in the world ...?' Amanda began wearily, then stopped as her mother turned horrified eyes on her.

'Amanda,' she said emotionally. 'Oh, dear God—the scandal—the disgrace! I can't believe it.'

'What can't you believe?' Amanda was totally bewildered.

Mrs Conroy thrust a paper at her with a trembling hand. 'Read it,' she said with a sob. 'See what you've done.'

The tabloid headlines were quite unequivocal. 'Rally-driver's heartbreak!' screamed one. And 'Jilted Nigel says, "I forgive her,"' another proclaimed.

Nausea rose in Amanda's throat. She whispered, 'He couldn't have done this. Oh, God, he couldn't ...'

She began to scan the first story with feverish concentration. 'While rally-driver Nigel Templeton was celebrating a personal best at Calthorpe this week, he was unaware that heartache awaited in his love-life,' the opening paragraph ran emotively. 'For his fiancé, lovely twenty-year-old Amanda Conroy, was enjoying a secret love-tryst with Nigel's own brother, Malory Templeton, millionaire owner of Templeton Laboratories. And yesterday, a stunned Nigel revealed that the couple intend to wed.'

'Oh, my God!' Amanda couldn't read any more.

Mrs Conroy was weeping openly. 'Poor Nigel, poor boy. No wonder you didn't want to apologise to him. You were too ashamed. Meeting his brother in "a hideaway love-nest".' She invested the words with horrified scorn, then struck the paper she was reading with her fist.

'Oh, you wicked girl,' she sobbed. 'Where did you go with him? Where was this dreadful place?'

Amanda said grimly, 'I presume they mean this house.'

Mrs Conroy clutched at her throat. 'You mean, you brought your—paramour here? You actually used my home for your sordid—your disgusting...'

'There's nothing disgusting or sordid about it.' Amanda gently shook her mother's arm. 'Mother— these stories are lies.'

'You mean you never met this man?'

'No.' Amanda swallowed. 'I did see him on Thursday. In fact, he spent the night here, but...'

'Then it's all true.' Her mother looked at her with tragic eyes. 'You brought him here. You——' She nerved herself. 'You—slept with him.'

Amanda groaned. 'Not in the way you think. I'd had a terrible day. I'd quarrelled with Nigel, and

Malory knew it. He just came to—keep me company. Then someone started ringing up, practising his heavy breathing, and my window got broken, so Malory and I finished up sharing the spare room, because I was too frightened to be on my own. But he never touched me. He just looked after me,' she added feebly.

Mrs Conroy snorted. 'A likely story! If it was all so innocent, why didn't you give Nigel a full explanation?'

Amanda flushed. 'Because I didn't think he deserved one,' she said in a constricted voice. She bit her lip. 'But Malory does. I'll have to talk to him before he sees these stories.'

Her mother laughed harshly. 'Are you quite mad? He's seen them already.' She read from her paper, '"At his Aylesford Green luxury residence, yesterday, Malory Templeton, thirty-two, said 'No comment'."'

She glared at Amanda. 'That's what guilty people say. Why didn't he deny these stories if they aren't true? Oh, just listen to this. "Nigel, white and shaken, said, 'I couldn't believe I'd lost her until she told me with her own lips that she was going to marry my brother. She was always against my rallying, and I can't blame her for choosing comfort and security with Malory. He's much richer than I can ever hope to be. I pray they'll both be happy together'."'

She shook her head. 'Poor boy. Poor, darling Nigel. So brave, wishing you well.'

'Is that what he's doing?' Amanda asked ironically. She rubbed her forehead with the back of her hand. 'Where are the road maps? I've got to get to Aylesford Green.'

'You won't go anywhere near that man,' Mrs Conroy said peremptorily. 'I shall get my solicitor to phone these papers tomorrow and issue a stringent denial, and then I shall speak to Nigel myself—tell him there's been a dreadful mistake...'

Amanda said quietly, 'Mother, if you do any such thing, I shall leave this house, and never come back. The papers got one thing right in all this. Nigel and I are finished. Nigel knows it, and that's why he's produced this—piece of spite.' She drew a breath. 'He said he'd make me sorry, and he has.'

Nigel had been very clever, she thought later as she drove through the lanes towards Aylesford Green. He'd presented her as an out-and-out gold-digger, and Malory as a wealthy dupe, while reserving for himself the role of deceived but noble innocent. Few people who read the stories would feel anything but compassion for him, betrayed at his moment of triumph.

It was raining when she reached the village. She parked her car by the green, and stared round at the pretty cottages which bordered it. There had been a smudgy picture of Malory's house in one of the papers, but she couldn't relate it to any of these. Eventually, she asked for directions from a man stalwartly walking his dog, and was guided out of the village on to a side road.

'It's set back a bit,' she was advised. 'Look out for double white gates.'

When she found them, Amanda drew her car up on the verge, and sat for a few moments, trying to marshal her thoughts. Or was she simply attempting to pluck up sufficient courage to walk up to the front door of the spacious brick and timber house she could just glimpse through the encircling trees? she asked herself derisively. It would serve her right if Malory refused point-blank to see her.

Only a matter of hours ago, he'd told her he was her friend, and they'd shaken hands on it. But today he might feel that friendship had its limitations.

She got stiffly out of the car and locked it. Well, she had no one but herself to blame for this fiasco. She'd made all the bullets for Nigel to fire with such lethal effect.

Her high-heeled boots scrunched over the wet gravel as she approached the front door, and rang the bell. Somewhere inside the house, a dog erupted into a tumult of barking, then quietened, obviously to order. The door opened, and a grey-haired woman in a neat dark overall looked at her enquiringly. 'May I help you, miss?'

'I'd like to see Dr Templeton, please.'

The woman gave her a formally regretful smile. 'I'm afraid Dr Templeton isn't seeing anyone today. You should direct any enquiries to the public relations department at the laboratories tomorrow.'

As she made to shut the door, Amanda said hastily, 'But I'm not a reporter. I'm Amanda Conroy, and I need to see Mal...Dr Templeton urgently.'

'Oh, Miss Conroy.' There was a wary note in the woman's voice. 'Come in, please. Dr Templeton has been expecting you.'

The hall was wide, with a flagged floor on which a Persian rug took pride of place. There was a Georgian table standing against one of the pale-washed walls holding a sunburst of chrysan-themums. Amanda was taken up two steps to double glass doors opening into a large drawing-room. Logs crackled in a grate on the wide hearth, and the room was filled with music—a woman's voice singing something dramatic and unfamiliar.

Malory was stretched out on one of the sofas which flanked the fireplace, but as Amanda came in he rose and walked over to the hi-fi system which occupied most of one wall, removing the record from the turntable.

He said laconically, 'The mad scene from *Lucia di Lammermoor*. It seemed—appropriate, somehow.' He looked past Amanda to his house-keeper. 'Could you manage some coffee for us, Mrs Priddy, please?'

'Of course, sir.' The doors closed behind her and they were alone together.

Malory said, 'Why don't you sit down, Amanda, before you fall down?'

She stumbled across to a sofa. Its cushions were as soft as thistledown, but they could have been a bed of nails as far as Amanda was concerned.

She said, 'I had to see you to apologise—to explain...'

He said quietly, 'When the press started calling, I was going to issue a categorical denial. Then something told me to wait. It seems I was right.'

She nodded wretchedly.

'So, what happened?'

'Nigel came back, after you'd gone. There was a scene, and he made some remark about us having——' she swallowed painfully '—having slept together. He was vile, and I lost my temper, and let him think it was true.'

He said, 'I suppose I should have allowed for the red in that hair of yours. So, does Nigel simply think I should do the honourable thing by marrying you, or is there still more?'

Amanda nodded again, her hands twisting and re-twisting in her lap. 'He said awful things about both of us. It was terrible. And then he made a gibe about—my marrying you.' A long pause. 'So I said I was going to.' She sank her teeth into her lower lip. 'It was just a way of scoring a point. Of getting rid of him. I never dreamed he'd do—this. Oh, God, it's all my fault!'

Malory said grimly, 'If you're expecting a chivalrous denial from me, then you're going to be disappointed. The only points you've scored are own goals. You've made us look fools, and worse than fools.'

She said, 'You should have denied everything.'

'And risked the papers discovering a story they could really get their teeth into?' he queried coolly. 'Have some sense. With luck, Nigel's masterly misrepresentation of the facts will be a brief sensation, and soon forgotten. The damage has been done now, and if we start issuing joint denials, it will simply re-focus attention on the whole mess. I imagine you don't want that?'

She shuddered. 'No.'

'Exactly. So if we go along with the story, it should die a natural death eventually.'

She made herself meet his gaze. 'What do you mean—go along with it?'

'It's quite simple,' he said. 'You've told the world, through Nigel, that you're going to marry me. So—marry me you will.'

CHAPTER FOUR

AMANDA sat staring at him for a long moment, then she said shakily, 'That mad scene you were listening to—is it infectious?'

He smiled faintly. 'I don't think so.'

'Then how can you possibly—possibly suggest such a thing? It's the craziest, most ridiculous idea I've ever heard!'

His brows lifted. 'But it's your own idea. You've proposed to me, Amanda, in the most public way you could have devised. Well, I'm accepting your proposal, that's all.'

She said huskily, 'But you can't—I didn't mean it.'

He gave her a meditative look. 'So what are you planning to do about it? Jilt me, as you seem to have jilted Nigel?' He shook his head. 'No way, my child. Whether you intended it or not, you've plunged me into the middle of a *cause célèbre*. It isn't a situation I appreciate, believe me.'

She said wretchedly, 'I know—and I'm so sorry.'

'It's a little late for regrets.' He spoke gently enough, but there was an implacable note in his voice. 'I abominate having my private life made public property, so this engagement stands as mutual camouflage until the necessity for it is past.'

Relief flooded over her in a great wave. 'Oh, you mean we should just *pretend*?'

'Well, I was hardly suggesting a headlong dash to the altar,' he said with faint hauteur. He gave her a level look. 'How has your mother reacted to all this?'

She groaned. 'Don't ask. She's in a terrible state. She idolised Nigel, of course, and insists on regarding all this as some kind of little local difficulty.'

'I presume you haven't told her the truth?'

'I couldn't,' she said bluntly.

He said rather wryly, 'I can appreciate that. So, how are you going to explain our engagement to her? Tell her I talked you into it against your better judgement—or that I swept you helplessly off your feet?'

'The first option, I presume,' she said. 'I don't think I could even convince myself of the second...' She stopped with a little gasp, realising what she'd said. 'I—I didn't mean...'

'It really doesn't matter,' he said pleasantly. 'Now, I think I hear Mrs Priddy bringing our coffee.'

'I ought to be getting back, actually.' Amanda was still hideously embarrassed by her gaffe. She didn't feel equal to a continued tête-à-tête over the coffee-cups.

'It's quite safe to accept my hospitality, Amanda.' His voice was dry. 'Nothing more will be forced on you—except, perhaps, Mrs Priddy's home-made shortbread. And Harvey's attentions, of course.'

'Harvey?' Amanda felt totally out of her depth.

'My dog. He got very wet when I took him out earlier, and he's been drying off in the kitchen.'

Malory smiled faintly. 'But he regards that as a kind of banishment, so no doubt he'll be hot on Mrs Priddy's heels.'

As the drawing-room doors opened to admit the housekeeper with her tray, a handsome Springer spaniel slid into the room in her wake, his tail a blur of quivering goodwill, his attitude tentative, as if unsure of his welcome. Malory snapped his fingers, and the dog went straight to him, sitting down obediently at his feet.

'He's been scratching at the door and whining these past ten minutes,' Mrs Priddy said dourly, as she put the tray down. 'I never did see a nosier dog.'

Malory laughed. 'He just likes to know what's going on, that's all.' He pulled gently at the dog's ears and Harvey moaned ecstatically. 'Go and meet Amanda, Harv, and remember your manners.'

Amanda held out her hand and Harvey sniffed it with a certain amount of reserve before submitting to having the top of his head stroked.

'He's a darling,' she said.

'I'm glad you approve—and that he seems to like you. That's quite an important hurdle,' Malory said, before adding casually to Mrs Priddy, 'Miss Conroy and I are going to be married.' He smiled at Amanda. 'Pour me some coffee, darling. I like very little cream, and no sugar.'

Amanda was horribly aware her jaw had dropped open, and closed it hastily.

Mrs Priddy said sedately, 'Well, the news isn't totally unexpected, sir, as you must know. George and I wish you every happiness, I'm sure.' She looked at Amanda. 'If you'd like to see over the house, miss, I'd be glad to show you.'

Amanda spilled some coffee into the saucer. 'Perhaps some other time,' she managed, and Mrs Priddy withdrew, clearly disappointed.

Amanda said heatedly, 'I wish you'd warned me you were going to say that. And was it strictly necessary?'

'Absolutely,' he said. 'This may be pretence, Amanda, but it has to be convincing. And it's something you're going to have to get used to.'

'Never!' she said fiercely, and Harvey backed away with a low, startled growl.

Malory grinned slightly. 'You're going to have to learn to control your temper in front of Harvey,' he said. 'He's far more sensitive than I am. Now, drink your coffee, and tell me what kind of a ring you'd like.'

'A ring?' she echoed helplessly. 'Surely we don't need to go to those lengths?'

'And have everyone think I'm a cheapskate? Shame on you.'

She said, 'It doesn't occur to you that I might not want to wear someone else's ring so soon?'

'It occurs. Perhaps you could consider, at the same time, my feelings about bestowing a ring on a woman who has no intention of becoming my wife.'

Again, Amanda detected that trace of steel beneath the equable tones. She said in a muffled voice, 'It's just—an impossible situation.'

'Only if you allow the surface details to weigh on you.' Malory drank some of his coffee. 'If you were playing a role on stage, you'd use the appropriate costume and props, wouldn't you? Well, look on your engagement ring in the same light.'

She bit her lip. 'One thing I can guarantee from all this. I'll never lose my temper again.' She poured herself some coffee, and took a piece of the shortbread which had accompanied it, as Malory had predicted.

As she nibbled on it, she found herself glancing around the room, assimilating her surroundings. It was a lovely room, she thought, and light years removed from the preternaturally tidy and soulless environment she'd pictured Malory purchasing for himself. It was light and airy, with its french windows opening on to lawns, now waterlogged. But in the summer it would be lovely to sit out on the grass under that tree, then wander in as the sun went down behind the distant copse...

She caught at herself. Long before the summer, she hoped she would have extricated herself from this hideous situation, although she had no idea what she would do next. Perhaps she would work abroad. The company which employed her had offices in Brussels and Geneva, and other girls had transferred successfully, sometimes for several years. She gave a faint sigh, and Malory looked at her interrogatively.

'What is it?'

'I'm just considering some of the options—when all this is over.'

'We have the next few weeks to negotiate first,' he said with a touch of grimness. 'Please don't say or do anything to make anyone think our engagement is less than the genuine article.'

She sighed again. 'I'll try.' She replaced her coffee-cup on the tray, and looked at the fire. 'There's one problem you don't seem to have considered,' she said stiltedly.

'What's that?'

'Well, Nigel has given everyone the impression that we're having some kind of raging affair.' She tried to speak lightly, and failed.

'It's not much of a problem,' he said slowly, 'unless you're afraid I intend to take advantage of the fact. I didn't realise I'd given that impression.'

'You haven't,' she said miserably. 'I don't even know why I mentioned it. My whole life seems to be upside-down these days.'

He smiled at her. 'Well, let's just say you have nothing to worry about.' He paused. 'I imagine an occasional peck on the cheek when other people are present is allowed?'

'I suppose it's unavoidable,' she admitted.

Malory laughed out loud. 'I'm glad I've never harboured any illusions about my sex appeal,' he remarked. 'Ten minutes with you, Amanda, would shatter them completely.'

'I didn't mean that the way it sounded, either,' she said flushing. She got to her feet. 'I really will go now, before I put my foot in it again.'

Malory rose, too. He said casually, 'You'd better write down your London address for me—and your telephone number at work.'

'Is that essential?'

'It's a fairly conventional request,' he returned with a touch of impatience. 'Your flatmates—the people you work with—will expect some kind of contact between us, however minimal.'

'Yes, of course,' she said reluctantly. She wrote down the necessary information on a page torn from her diary, and gave it to him. 'How long do you think we'll have to maintain this charade?'

He shrugged. 'Until our supposed romance is such stale news that we can part without causing a flicker of interest in the gutter press.'

She looked at him uncertainly. 'And if Nigel won't let it die?'

'Nigel won't have the choice,' he said. 'Anyway, he has a rally in Sweden coming up quite soon. That should absorb his attention.'

'I suppose so.' She was silent for a moment, then said stumblingly, 'At the risk of repeating myself, I really am very sorry about involving you in all this.' She gave a wavering smile. 'You must wish you'd let me jump.'

'The only difference would have been that we would both have got very wet.' His tone was matter of fact. 'Stop blaming yourself, Amanda. Being exposed for the first time to the malicious side of Nigel's nature can be quite a shock to the system. It's hardly surprising you didn't behave rationally.'

'How nice to be able to analyse the situation so accurately,' Amanda said sourly as she walked to the door. 'Don't you ever forget you're a scientist?'

'Not very often.' He didn't sound in the least put out. In fact, he was smiling. 'Goodbye, Amanda. I'll be in touch.'

Amanda's head was whirling as she drove home. She supposed she should be grateful that Malory hadn't lost his temper and given her the tongue-lashing she knew she deserved, but in an odd way she would have preferred a storm of anger. Because the alternative was infinitely worse.

Of course, it made a kind of weird sense. Fighting the newspaper stories would only attract more unwelcome attention to them. A tacit acceptance of the situation seemed to be the answer.

But being forced to masquerade, even on a temporary basis, as Malory's fiancée was a distasteful prospect. After all, in spite of everything they'd been through together, he was still an almost total stranger to her, and what she did know about him, she didn't particularly like, she told herself roundly. His cool composure got right under her skin. But there was more to it than that. Under the politely civilised exterior he presented, there were signs of a formidable personality, she suspected.

She sighed. She would never call Malory a non-entity again, she thought uneasily.

And the next few weeks promised to be the most difficult of her life.

Amanda tucked the last file back in the drawer, closed the filing cabinet and locked it with a feeling of relief. It had been a very long day. Jeffrey Lane, her boss, had returned that morning from his vacation, and set the whole building by the ears. Everyone knew that Jeffrey hated holidays, and only went on them because his wife insisted. He invariably returned in a foul temper, bursting with frustrated energy, and this time had proved no exception. But every cloud had its silver lining, and Jeffrey's determination to turn the company inside out had, at least, served to distract people's attention from her rift with Nigel and its aftermath.

Secure and happy in her engagement, she had never realised before what a hotbed of gossip Lane Gerstein was. She'd looked on work as a sanctuary—an escape from her mother's querulous and unceasing criticism—but it had proved the opposite. Since her return, she'd found herself exposed to every kind of innuendo and speculation. Only her pride had prevented her from reporting sick and going to ground at the flat.

Yet there wasn't a great deal of peace there, either. Fiona and Maggie clearly thought she was mad to have split from Nigel, although Jane's reaction had been kinder and more tactful. But there were altogether too many sudden and awkward silences each time she entered the kitchen or the living-room. And, since Malory's unexpected announcement of their engagement in two of the leading dailies, and a short-lived revival of press interest in her love-life, it had been impossible to confide in her companions—even in Jane.

Anyway, she wasn't sure she wanted to admit to anyone what a total fool she'd made of herself. In retrospect, she was frankly appalled by her behaviour, and thankful that no one else knew what a hash she'd made of things. She bit her lip. No one, of course, except Malory Templeton.

Since her return to London, he had telephoned twice, once at the office, and once at the flat, inviting her to meet him, but each time she'd made an excuse and, thankfully, he now seemed to think that honour had been satisfied by his going through the motions of acting the attentive fiancé, and was leaving her in peace.

Going abroad, even on a temporary basis, was beginning to seem an increasingly attractive prospect. If she went where she was completely unknown, she might be able to start dragging the rags of her life together again.

When she got outside the building, Amanda found to her annoyance that it had been snowing slightly, and the traffic was in turmoil as a result. She had to queue for ages for a bus, and when it came it crawled along while Amanda sat, hunched and miserable in her seat, gazing unseeingly through the splashed window.

The others were already home when she got to the flat. She was unzipping her boots in the hall when Jane appeared, grinning at her.

'Had a nice day?'

Amanda shuddered. 'Can we just draw a veil over the whole painful subject?' she appealed. 'What's for supper?'

Jane grimaced. 'Fiona's macaroni cheese for us.' Her eyes twinkled. 'What you might be having is open to speculation.' With the air of a conjuror producing a rabbit from a hat, she handed Amanda a bouquet of long-stemmed pink roses which she'd been hiding behind her back. The accompanying card said, 'Dinner tonight', and was signed with a single 'M'.

'They were waiting when I got back,' Jane said triumphantly. 'Aren't they absolutely gorgeous?'

'Why—yes,' Amanda agreed weakly.

'Well, put them in water, and then go and get changed,' Jane urged. 'You're awfully late, and he could be here at any minute.' She lowered her voice. 'And you don't surely want to leave him to Maggie's tender mercies. The last thing he'll want to hear is what swine you've both been to poor old Nigel. And she's quite capable of saying it, and more.' She paused. 'Hey, love, don't look so stricken. I'll fend her off if you're not ready in time.'

Amanda gave her a subdued smile. 'Thanks.' She held out the roses. 'Could you see to these for me?'

Jane's brows rose. 'If you like, but I'd have thought you'd want to arrange them yourself.' She gave Amanda a searching look. 'You're all right, are you? You haven't picked up this virus thing that's going the rounds?'

Amanda shook her head, and went off to the bedroom they shared. She was still holding Malory's card, and she put it slowly down on the dressing-table. This time, it seemed, she was not being given any option. She wondered if he'd penned the message himself. The handwriting looked firm and uncompromising, especially the single initial.

She bit her lip. This wasn't so much an invitation as a statement, and she resented it. It was irksome, too, to realise that Malory wasn't prepared to take the hint after all, and stay away from her.

She opened her half of the wardrobe and ran an indifferent look along its hanging rail. Perhaps she should have latched on to Jane's suggestion about the virus, and got the girls to make her excuses when Malory arrived.

On the other hand, she would only be delaying the inevitable. It was obvious that Malory intended to see her, and the best thing would be to get it over with as quickly as possible.

She had a quick bath in the small, cramped bathroom, crouching under the usual rack of damp tights and undies, then dressed swiftly and unadventurously in a silky black dress, long-sleeved and high-necked. She put on a modicum of make-up, and brushed her hair loose on her shoulders, before giving herself a swift, clinical inspection in the mirror. She looked neat, if unexciting, she thought. And if Malory expected more, then he was going to be disappointed.

She was tucking her purse and compact into her bag, when Jane stuck her head round the door. 'He's here,' she whispered. 'And Maggie's moving in.'

Amanda reached the living-room in time to hear Maggie say aggressively, 'Don't you believe in animal rights, Dr Templeton?'

'I certainly believe in human rights.' Malory sounded cool and faintly bored.

'But you test your drugs on helpless creatures in your laboratories.'

'When necessary, and under humane conditions.'

'You think that justifies the suffering you cause?'

'What I try and achieve is an alleviation of suffering for my fellow men,' Malory said flatly.

'Would you care to volunteer to replace the animals used in tests?'

'That's a ridiculous idea!' Maggie said hotly. 'What I want is to see all testing ended by law.'

He said quietly, 'Try telling that to a mother whose child has leukemia.' He looked at the doorway, and saw Amanda standing there. His smile was wintry. 'So, there you are, darling.'

'Yes.' Amanda flushed as she walked forward to join him. He bent slightly towards her, and she lifted her face perfunctorily for the brief, cool brush of his lips on hers.

As he lifted his head, he looked into her eyes, his own gaze warm and faintly teasing. 'Missed me?'

Her blush deepened, and she murmured something incoherent. She could see Maggie and Fiona exchanging glances, and Jane's bewildered frown as she slid her arm through his, and tugged him towards the door.

As they descended the stairs to street level, she said, 'I think you missed your vocation. You'd have made a good actor.'

'Well, one of us needs to be.' His tone was slightly caustic. 'You treated me as if I was Marley's Ghost.'

She realised she was still holding his arm, and released it abruptly. She said tautly, 'I wasn't expecting to see you. Your summons surprised me.'

Malory gave her an ironic look. 'Did you think you could avoid me for ever?'

She shrugged. 'There's no harm in hoping. I mean, there's no real reason for you to—put in any personal appearances in my life. I thought I could just—pretend to see you when I went home at weekends.'

'But you didn't go home last weekend,' he pointed out gently.

'No.' Amanda sighed. 'Mother's still being difficult.'

'I'm sorry to hear it,' he said, 'but the fact is you're not the only one with a life, and I do require you to put in the occasional—er, personal appearances at my side.'

She shot him a dismayed look. 'When?'

'In two weeks' time at the company dinner,' he said promptly. 'You can manage that, I hope. The staff are looking forward to meeting you.'

They had reached his car. Amanda stood her ground. 'I can't,' she said baldly. 'It's quite impossible. I can't go and foist myself on all these people under false pretences.'

'There's nothing false about it.' Malory unlocked the passenger door for her. 'Our engagement is quite official.' He added, dead-pan, 'I saw it in *The Times*.'

'And so did I.' Amanda found she was sitting in the car without really knowing how she got there. 'That was an unnecessary refinement, surely?'

'I don't think so.' His mouth twisted slightly. 'I felt it gave a veneer of respectability to a rather ramshackle arrangement.'

'So is this why you're taking me to dinner—to ask me to go to your company party? Surely a phone call would have been sufficient?'

'Probably, but I felt it was time I checked up on you.' The purr of the ignition springing to life muffled Amanda's snort of indignation. 'You've lost some weight, which you can't afford to do,' he went on almost casually. 'So a square meal is clearly a good idea. Besides, I have another reason for seeking you out.'

She said pettishly, 'You take a hell of a lot for granted. Suppose I'd had another date this evening?'

'Then you'd have broken it,' he said cheerfully. 'I think a fiancé has priority, don't you?'

'I think you're carrying this charade to ridiculous lengths,' Amanda said shortly, and lapsed into silence.

The restaurant he took her to lay in a quiet side street. It was small, French, and obviously exclusive. It was also clear that Malory was a regular and valued patron.

Amanda noticed, too, that there were no prices in the leather-bound menu she was solicitously handed.

Simply reading it was a mouth-watering experience. Amanda ate *mousseline* of sole, followed by duck breast cooked with mangoes, and finished with strawberries and *crème Chantilly* served in a basket of wafer-thin sweet pastry. As coffee and Armagnac were brought to the table, she sat back with a sigh of repletion.

'That was a marvellous meal. Thank you.'

'You never came here with Nigel?'

She shook her head. 'He likes bigger restaurants—places where...' She hesitated.

'Places where he can see and be seen,' Malory supplied, and she nodded.

'Is that what you prefer?' he asked. 'We could have gone to Langans if you'd wished...'

'Oh, no,' she denied hastily. 'I—I love it here.'

'Good.' He smiled at her. 'At least we have one thing in common.'

'Yes.' Amanda's voice held a trace of uncertainty. She glanced at her watch. 'It's getting quite late...'

'Yes, isn't it?' he said cordially. 'All right, Amanda, I'll take you safely back to your flat. But first we have a small piece of business to settle.'

'We do?'

Malory said with faint asperity, 'Don't look so stricken. It isn't anything very formidable.' He took a small velvet-covered box from his pocket, and passed it across the table to her. 'This is for you. My choice, I'm afraid, as you've proved so elusive over the past fortnight.'

Amanda opened the box with trepidation, and gasped. She was looking at an exquisite square-cut emerald, surrounded by diamonds.

'But I can't wear this.'

'You think it will be the wrong size? Well, that can easily be altered.'

'No, I didn't mean that. It—it's too much—too beautiful. It must have cost a fortune. You shouldn't have done it.'

'Actually, it belonged to my mother. Does that make you feel better about it?'

If anything, it made her feel worse. 'Then it's an heirloom...'

'Not really.' He paused. 'Anyway, a lot of heir-looms go out on temporary loan, so look at it in that light. Besides, beautiful jewellery needs to be worn, not kept locked in safe deposits.' He took her hand, and gently but firmly slid the ring over her knuckle. 'There—it does fit, Cinderella.'

It was about as different from the ring Nigel had given her as it was possible to get, she thought helplessly, and she guessed that was quite deliberate.

She said in a muffled voice, 'I'll take care of it.'

'Just enjoy wearing it.' He was still holding her fingers lightly. 'It suits the shape of your hand.'

She gave him an embarrassed smile, and de-tached herself. 'I really should go.'

Malory nodded and signalled to the waiter.

The homeward journey was a silent one. Amanda's thoughts were confused, but the shape of the emerald under her questing fingers was only too real.

When the car stopped, she said stiltedly, 'Thank you for a—nice evening.'

'I'm glad it wasn't the ordeal you anticipated.'

She couldn't see if he was smiling or not. A pre-vious omission had occurred to her. 'And—thank you for the flowers.'

'Did you like them?'

'Well——' Amanda hesitated. 'Actually, I thought they were a bit over the top.'

He was definitely amused now. 'Oh, I think I'm permitted the odd romantic gesture—don't you?'

Amanda didn't know what to say. The interior of the car seemed suddenly altogether too dark, too confined—too intimate for this kind of conversation. It occurred to her, tremulously, that Malory might have a different kind of romantic gesture in mind altogether—and that, if he did try and take her in his arms, she wouldn't know quite how to react.

He'd bought her dinner, her mind ran feverishly, and given—lent her this exquisite ring. She could hardly haul off and slap his face if he kissed her.

The silence between them seemed endless. Amanda was tense, waiting for him to reach for her...

But he didn't. When he spoke, his tone was matter of fact. 'I'll ring you in a few days about the company party. Now, I'd better get you safely indoors.'

Outside the flat, Amanda found her hand shaking as she fitted her key into the lock.

'Thank you again.' Her voice sounded higher-pitched than usual—taut. And it was ridiculous to be so nervous. Malory was doing nothing more threatening than watching her struggles with the key.

'Let me.' He took the key from her and unlocked the door. 'I won't come in,' he went on. 'I can't face another harangue on behalf of Animal Lib.'

Amanda forced a small smile. 'Maggie's current boyfriend is some kind of activist and it always affects her. The last one was heavily into CND,' she added, stumbling a little over the words.

He said lazily, 'What a hectic existence she must lead.' He put a finger under Amanda's chin, tilting her face to meet his gaze. His voice gentled. 'Calm down, darling. There's nothing to be afraid of.' He released her and gently turned away. 'I'll be in touch,' he added almost casually.

The hall was in darkness. Amanda leaned against the closed door, her breathing as rapid as if she'd been taking part in some kind of race. He was perfectly correct, she thought. There had been nothing to fear, after all. It had all been in her own mind.

And that should have been the most tremendous relief.

So why, therefore, did she feel as if it had been a total anticlimax?

CHAPTER FIVE

'THAT,' Jane said, 'is the most fantastic dress.'

'Do you think it's all right?' Amanda surveyed herself in the mirror. 'It's not too...'

'Far from it,' Jane assured her. 'It's obvious you're not wearing a bra, of course, because the thing has hardly any back, but that's the only way you can tell. That high halter front is very discreet. And I love all those masses of tiny pleats in the skirt.'

'Culottes, actually.' Amanda demonstrated. She frowned a little. 'It isn't at all the kind of thing I intended to buy. It's far too extravagant. I meant to get something that would do later on, when...' She stopped hastily, aware she'd been about to venture into indiscretion. But Jane was clearly too fascinated by the golden shimmer of the new dress to have noticed.

'Live a little,' she advised airily. 'After all, you're marrying a very wealthy man.'

Amanda bit her lip. 'I suppose so.' She hesitated. 'I ought to explain, but I can't...'

'You don't have to,' Jane said robustly. 'Anyone's entitled to change her mind, and it's far better to do it before you're married than afterwards.' It was her turn to pause. 'And, actually, I was never Nigel's greatest fan.'

Amanda stared at her. 'But you never said anything,' she protested.

Jane shrugged. 'What could I say? You seemed so knocked out by him that I didn't think you'd listen, and anyway, it was none of my business.' She grimaced drolly. 'Maggie's Tim doesn't inspire me with admiration, either.'

Amanda smiled wryly. 'I'm not surprised.'

'And I thought your Malory handled her very well the other night,' Jane went on. 'She was being terribly aggressive, and he was polite, but remote.' She slanted a look at Amanda. 'He's not an easy man to get to know, is he?'

'No,' Amanda agreed, her voice colourless. 'Do you think I need more blusher?'

Jane inspected her minutely. 'Not a scrap. You look really good. Have a nice party, and a lovely weekend. You're going home, aren't you?'

'Yes, straight from the party.' Amanda picked up the pleated cape that matched her dress, and put it round her shoulders. Going to the cottage was a decision which had been pretty much forced on her. She'd had a week of reproachful phone calls from her mother, and had bowed to their pressure, even though she knew Mrs Conroy still hadn't forgiven her for breaking off with Nigel, and the resulting publicity.

'Another reporter rang up only yesterday,' had been Mrs Conroy's parting shot. 'Asking if you and that man had set the date yet. I told him I hadn't the least idea.'

Amanda had been left staring in a startled way at the receiver. The newspapers weren't ready yet to relinquish their grip on the story, it seemed, and this depressed her.

As she drove with Malory to the big country hotel where the dinner dance was being held, she said abruptly, 'The press have been on to my mother, asking when we're going to be married.'

'They phoned me, too.' He didn't seem perturbed, she noted crossly.

'So, what did you tell them?'

'That we were making no announcement at present.' He paused. 'That seemed to cover a variety of possibilities.'

'I suppose so.' Amanda sighed. 'I hoped they'd have decided to leave us alone by now.'

He said drily, 'How very optimistic.' He slanted a glance at her. 'Are you really so desperate to be free of all this?'

'Of course. I want to find another job—build a new life for myself.' She knew she sounded defensive. 'Isn't that natural?'

'Perfectly. But I'm afraid, for the time being, you'll just have to be patient.' He sounded bored. 'In fact, we both will.'

Amanda said a subdued, 'Yes,' and relapsed into silence.

He was in an odd mood this evening, she thought, stealing a covert, sideways glance at him. He'd admired her dress, but courteously, as if his thoughts were elsewhere. Perhaps he was tired, too, of all this pretence, and longing to return to normality, and his civilised, rather solitary existence.

Or perhaps, she thought later, he'd merely been thinking what lay in store for them that evening.

Her mouth ached with smiling, and her fingers were sore from some of the over-enthusiastic hand-shaking she'd been subjected to as she stood at Malory's side in the receiving line. And the worst of it was, everyone seemed so genuinely pleased for them both, unstinting in their good wishes.

He has no right to put me through all this, Amanda fulminated silently.

She glanced up and saw him watching her, his gaze ironic, as if he'd guessed what she was thinking. And, of course, he had every right. After all, she had created this entire mess single-handed. She'd involved him in the kind of notoriety he most abhorred. The least she could do was stand by him tonight.

She bit her lip. And for as long as it took...

She could comfort herself with the reflection that she was looking good. She could see it in the eyes of the men she was introduced to. They envied Malory, and the knowledge warmed her. It occurred to her that, when she'd been out with Nigel, she'd been the one who was envied.

And she seemed to be passing muster with the women, too. She'd overheard a snatch of conversation in the powder-room.

'It seemed so unlike him,' someone was saying to a friend. 'But she's lovely looking, isn't she? You can understand him losing his head over her.'

The friend's reply was indistinguishable, but seemed to be in broad agreement.

If only you knew! Amanda thought.

At dinner, she found herself stationed next to one of Malory's chief chemists, a pleasant-faced young man with thinning hair and a ready smile. They talked generalities for a while, then she asked him about his work and saw his face brighten.

Among other things, he told her, they were working on a drug called Chromazyn, which they hoped would relieve arthritis sufferers.

'It's something I feel strongly about,' he said. 'I had a grandmother I adored, and she was nearly crippled with arthritis during her last years. I want Chromazyn to work for her sake, I suppose. A few doctors have started to prescribe it already, monitored by us, of course, in case of side-effects. But, so far, it seems to be going well. I'm surprised Malory hasn't told you about it.' He grinned at her. 'But I expect you have other things to discuss.'

Amanda made some non-committal response, and changed the subject. She supposed that, if her engagement to Malory was to continue for any length of time, she would have to take a surface interest at least in what went on at the laboratories.

When dinner was over, she danced with everyone who asked her, responding demurely to some of the heavy-handed gallantry to which she was subjected, particularly by the older men. She began to wish she'd worn something rather less striking. She felt like a bird of paradise who'd fluttered inadvertently into a dovecote.

It was almost a relief to find herself claimed by Malory.

'Congratulations,' he murmured in her ear. 'You've taken them all by storm.'

'Oh, don't,' she said, distressed. 'I feel such a fraud.'

'Then, don't,' he said. 'You've provided them with a far more enjoyable evening than they've ever had before—endless food for speculation.'

'And you don't mind that?'

'Not really. You see, they're my people. There's very little malice there.'

'You're lucky,' she said bitterly. 'It's been absolute hell at my office.' She forced a smile. 'It's only when you've made a mistake that you find out what people really think of you.'

Malory said drily, 'That can sometimes be quite comforting.'

She could see that it could be—for him. She'd already discovered through the course of the evening how highly Malory was regarded and respected by his workforce. But then, she thought sourly, he paid their salaries. And immediately castigated herself silently for being a bitch.

He was certainly, she thought, a much better dancer than she would ever have given him credit for.

She said rather challengingly, 'You must hate this kind of music.'

His brows lifted. 'What makes you say that?'

'Well—it's a long way from Donizetti.'

'There's room for both.' He gave her a long look. 'One of these days I'll have to prove to you that I'm not as hidebound as you think.'

She said rather too hurriedly, 'I'll take your word for it,' and felt a stab of relief that the dance was coming to an end. But to her surprise, as the tempo of the music slowed and became dreamy, Malory pulled her back into his arms, his hands sliding down round her waist to hold her closer.

'Don't make a fuss,' he directed under his breath. 'It's only what they'll expect of us, after all. Put your arms round my neck.'

Stiffly and reluctantly, she did as she was told. It annoyed her that he could be relaxed and casual about it all. She stole a furtive glance at her wrist-watch. Suddenly, she couldn't wait for the evening to be over.

But, even when the dancing was finished, there were other formalities to be gone through, and goodbyes to be said. It was ages before she sat beside Malory in his car, speeding quietly through the darkness.

She sighed quietly, and he gave her a swift sideways glance. 'Did you hate it all very much?'

'No, I didn't,' she discovered to her surprise. 'Everyone was so kind, and welcoming.' She added awkwardly, 'Any problems were all in my own head.'

'I think that applies to most of us.'

She said stiltedly, 'It must have been difficult for you, too.' She thought of Clare, whom Malory had probably hoped to present to his workforce as his future wife at that very party. 'You must have thought how very—different everything could have been. I keep forgetting I'm not the only injured party.'

'There's little point in endlessly going over what might have been,' he said drily. 'I've learned to resign myself. I advise you to do the same.'

'Maybe it will be easier with a change of scene.'

'You're planning to go away?' he asked with polite interest. 'Any particular destination in mind?'

'Not yet. I can't make any firm arrangements really, until all this is over.'

'Well, you shouldn't have much longer to endure it,' he said.

'I hope not.' She hesitated. 'I was thinking of going abroad, if I can get the same kind of job.'

'I might be able to help there. I have various contacts in the pharmaceutical industries, if that appeals to you.'

'I'll bear it in mind.' She wouldn't, of course; the last thing she wanted was to be beholden to Malory Templeton. But at least he wasn't putting any obstacles in her way, or insisting she serve some minimum term as his fiancée, she thought. In fact, he seemed almost anxious to speed her on her way. But even that was understandable after the embarrassment she'd caused him. Playing her part correctly this evening might have made up a little for that, or so she hoped. However, she wanted no more such evenings.

Malory parked outside the cottage and took her weekend case from the boot while Amanda found her door key.

'Thank you.' She held out her hand for the case, then hesitated. 'Would you like a nightcap before you go?'

'No alcohol,' he said, 'but I would appreciate some coffee.'

Amanda was completely taken aback. She'd expected him to make some courteous excuse and be on his way. But she could hardly withdraw the offer now, so, mutely, she allowed him to follow her into the cottage.

She'd half hoped her mother would still be downstairs, but the drawing-room was in darkness, except for the logs smouldering quietly behind the spark-guard.

Amanda gave a small, silent sigh. In the old days, Mrs Conroy would have been up, waiting eagerly for all the details of the evening—what had been worn, eaten, said and done. The fact that she'd gone to bed was a sign of her continuing displeasure.

She switched on the lamps and added another log to the fire, before going to the kitchen to prepare the coffee. She glanced at the percolator, then hunched a shoulder. He could have instant, and like it.

Malory was occupying the armchair, very much at his ease, when Amanda returned.

'This is very kind of you.'

She wondered if she could detect a note of irony in his voice, and dismissed the idea. She handed him his mug, then seated herself on the sofa in a swirl of silky gold pleats, yawning ostentatiously as she reached for her own coffee.

'You'd never have made an actress if you're exhausted after one performance,' Malory commented.

'Then it's lucky I had no such ambition,' Amanda retorted.

'So, what did you want from life? Or was your only horizon a secretarial post, followed by a suitable marriage?'

'Of course not.' He made it sound so appallingly conventional, she thought vexedly. And who was he to talk, anyway? 'And I'm not a secretary. I'm a personal assistant,' she added defensively.

'Ah,' he said gravely. 'That, of course, makes a difference.'

'Well, it does to me.' Amanda set down her mug with a definite thump. 'It's all right for you to sit there, being lordly, but we didn't all have an enormous company handed to us on a plate.'

'Neither did I. Believe it or not, Amanda, I had to fight tooth and nail for everything I wanted. It was a valuable lesson about life.'

'Which you are presumably handing on. I'm sure you mean well, but I'm really not in the market for fatherly advice.' She'd intended to sound crushing, and was totally disconcerted by his shout of laughter. She cast a nervous glance ceiling-wards. 'Oh, do be quiet, or you'll wake my mother, and she'll wonder why you're still here.'

He was still grinning. 'And what will she do? Come rushing down to protect your virtue from my fell designs?'

'Hardly,' Amanda said crossly. 'Anyway, you haven't got any fell designs.'

There was an odd loaded silence, then he said quite gently, 'Amanda, you can't possibly be that naïve. You're a beautiful, desirable girl. There wasn't a man in that room tonight who wasn't wondering what it would be like to make love to you.'

She cast him an edged, nervous glance. 'Please— don't say things like that.'

'You'd prefer me to pretend it had never crossed my mind?' He shook his head. 'That would be dishonest.'

'The whole situation's dishonest.' She was startled to hear an almost desperate note in her own voice. 'You're not in love with me—you know you're not . . . And I don't care for you.'

'What difference does that make?' He sounded amused. 'We're not talking about a lifetime's commitment, but a brief interlude of what used to be called dalliance, I think. Quite permissible, even between comparative strangers.'

He rose to his feet, putting down his coffee and, before Amanda could resist, had sat down beside her, lifting her on to his lap with one smooth, forceful movement which totally circumvented any avoiding action on her part.

She said in a small, breathless voice, 'Let go of me.'

'In my own good time.' Malory lifted a finger and stroked an errant tress of hair back from her temple. 'When you've thanked me politely for your pleasant evening.'

'Not like this.' Even when they'd danced earlier, they hadn't been as intimately close as they were now, Amanda realised, her heart jerking at her ribcage. She could feel the warmth of his breath on her cheek—knew that she would only have to turn her head a fraction to taste his mouth against hers.

'Stop panicking, darling,' he advised coolly. 'I've never belonged to the school of thought which considers a girl's body an appropriate repayment for dinner and a bottle of wine.'

'No?' She'd never sounded so gauche and unsure of herself in her life, especially now that his thumb was tracing the curve of her averted cheek, the line of her jaw, sending odd little shivers through her body. 'You—you must be very unusual.'

'Why? Because I prefer the pleasure of a woman's company—and the possibility of future delight— to immediate gratification?' Malory shook his head slowly. 'I'm not that eccentric. And I don't believe in instant bliss, either,' he added drily.

Amanda swallowed. This was the last kind of conversation she'd ever expected to have—wanted to have—with Malory. Oh, why in the world hadn't she simply said goodnight to him on the doorstep? she wailed silently.

'No comment?' he asked, as the silence lengthened.

Amanda rallied her forces. 'It's really none of my business,' she said, trying to sound dismissive. 'And it's getting awfully late...'

'So it is,' he said. 'Then I'll waste no more time.' His fingers closed on her chin, turning her face inexorably to his. He was smiling as he kissed her.

His mouth was warm and gentle, but also very determined as it moved on hers. She couldn't struggle—he was holding her too closely in the circle of his arms for that—but she protested silently by keeping her lips firmly closed against his insistence.

In spite of his apparent assurances, his remark about 'future delight' disturbed her, and she wanted in no way to encourage him to think that she might ever be even remotely willing...

Nevertheless, she could not deny that the intimate proximity of their bodies, not to mention the lingering sensuousness of his kiss, was having an inevitable effect on her senses. Her entire body seemed to be tingling, coming to life, no matter how much mental resistance she could summon up, and she was shocked by her own reaction.

When he'd made her put her arms round him on the dance-floor earlier, her fingers had accidentally brushed the hair at the nape of his neck, and the contact with its crisp thickness had shocked her like an electric current. Now, she knew an impulse to touch his hair again, to lift her hands to his head, and hold him, and the strength of this response alarmed her.

Even as she tensed against it, Malory's own hand moved from its gentle stroking of her throat, down the bare curve of her shoulder and arm to her waist. His fingers splayed across her ribcage, moving in small rhythmic circles on the golden silk which veiled her skin.

He lifted his head, and looked down into her eyes. 'Was that so terrifying?' he whispered with faint mockery.

She was lost for an answer. On the face of it, she wasn't threatened at all. Even the way he was touching her now was perfectly circumspect, his hand remaining at a discreet, if narrow, distance from the curve of her breast.

At the same time, she was beginning to realise that those gentle circling movements had an eroticism all their own, because they pulled delicately at the silken fabric which covered her breasts, setting up a sweet and subtle friction against the sensitive peaks.

Suddenly, it was becoming difficult to breathe. A languour had invaded her limbs, and there was an odd drumming in her ears, as if she'd tuned in to the inward pulse of her own blood. She could feel her nipples hardening involuntarily against the thin bodice.

She wanted to say, 'Don't,' but no words would come. Not even when she felt Malory's other hand lightly stroking her stockinged leg from ankle to knee, brushing aside the myriad pleats of the culotte skirt as he did so.

As his head bent towards her again, she yielded weakly, her lips parting in anticipation and a shamed need. This time, when he kissed her, there would be no barrier to any of the intimacies he sought.

But instead, Amanda felt the swift brush of his lips on her forehead, before he lifted her briskly off his knee on to the cushions she'd occupied previously.

He said pleasantly, 'I think it's time I left,' and got to his feet, straightening his tie, and raking a hand through his hair.

Amanda was suddenly, horribly aware that she was sprawled there, gaping at him, and jack-knifed into a sitting position.

He added lightly, 'You show your gratitude quite delightfully.'

Before she could say or do anything, he picked up his coat, walked to the door, and went out, closing it quietly behind him. A moment later, she heard the front door shut, too.

She sat where she was, staring after him, telling herself she would wake soon and find the entire events of the past half-hour a preposterous dream.

And then she caught sight of the carriage clock on the mantelpiece, and that galvanised her into action. If her mother woke now, and found she was still downstairs, she would be bound to come down, and Amanda was in no state to face any kind of inquisition. As she got to her feet, she found her legs were trembling so much they would hardly support her.

She moved the guard in front of the fire, and as she turned she caught a glimpse of herself in the ornamental antique mirror which ran along the wall above the sofa. In spite of herself, a little cry escaped her.

She'd thought Malory's last remark had referred to the fact that he'd enjoyed kissing her. But now she looked at herself, and saw what he had seen— the flush of excitement along her cheekbones, the eyes drowsy with awakened desire, the reddened, parted lips and, most damning of all evidence, the erect and swollen nipples clearly outlined under the thin dress.

And his comment took on a new and shaming significance.

Amanda lifted her hands and pressed them to her burning face.

How could I? she wept inwardly. Oh, God, how could I?

CHAPTER SIX

AMANDA stayed in bed until late the following morning, remaining hunched in a pretence of sleep even when she heard her mother enter with a cup of tea.

She could still find no adequate explanation for her conduct. It wasn't even as if she fancied—horrible word!—Malory. He wasn't her type, and anyway she was still hopelessly, wretchedly in love with Nigel. She sighed, burying her face in the pillow. She despised herself for that as well. After all, she now had no illusions left about him. He'd seen to that himself.

But neither the knowledge of that, nor the passage of time, could alleviate the hurt inside her, or that swift, stomach-churning, heart-leaping stab of excitement and yearning which assailed her whenever she thought of him. And she thought of him more often than she wanted to.

Which made her behaviour in Malory's arms all the more inexplicable. It wasn't what he'd done, either. It was what she'd found herself wanting him to do that made her writhe with embarrassment in the cold light of day. And the crowning humiliation was that it had been Malory himself who'd called the halt. Which proved, apart from anything else, that he'd been by no means as carried away as she was.

Amanda hit the pillow a blow with her clenched fist, and decided she had better get dressed.

She found Mrs Conroy sitting in the kitchen, listening to Radio Four and cleaning some silver—one of the few household tasks she did not allocate to her daily.

'So there you are, dear.' Her mother's voice sounded awkward and rather strained. 'Was it a nice party?'

'Very nice.' Just don't ask me about its aftermath, thought Amanda frantically.

'Are you going out today?'

'No, I don't think so.'

Mrs Conroy's face brightened. 'That's nice,' she said. 'It's so long since you've been down here and we've had the chance to talk—really talk.'

Amanda groaned inwardly. If a Trappist convent had beckoned at that moment, she would have joined it gladly.

'We're having sole *Véronique* for lunch,' Mrs Conroy went on, clearly warming to the idea of the day's tête-à-tête. 'Why don't we make it a real celebration and dress up a little?' She gave Amanda's jeans and sweater a charmingly disparaging glance. 'Wouldn't that be fun?'

'Perhaps I'll change later,' Amanda said. 'I might spend an hour in the garden.'

'Oh, not today, surely. It's certain to rain.' Mrs Conroy gave her an appealing look. 'Why don't you wear that lovely green dress I bought you, and your pearl ear-rings? I'm so tired of seeing you in those scruffy jeans.'

Amanda sighed. 'And I'm so tired of wearing smart clothes in London,' she returned ruefully. 'Can't I celebrate and be relaxed at the same time?'

'Amanda, dear—to please me?'

Amanda was not an admirer of her mother's little-girl mood, but it was certainly preferable to the martyred silences of recent times, so she stifled a sigh and got to her feet. 'All right,' she said resignedly. 'I'll put on a dress.'

'And some make-up?'

'Be content with the dress,' Amanda retorted as she went back into the hall.

She saw the drawing-room door standing open, and a thought struck her. Wasn't there a Concise Oxford Dictionary in the small bookcase near the window?

Indeed there was, but it brought her no particular comfort. Some of the meanings attributed to 'dalliance' were 'to amuse oneself' and 'to coquet with temptation'.

His and her definitions, Amanda thought, grinding her teeth before ramming the inoffensive book back on the shelf. It was at that moment that she heard the telephone ring. She got to the door, but her mother had already forestalled her, and was listening intently to whatever the caller had to say.

Amanda heard her say, 'Yes—in about an hour.' Then, 'Of course I haven't said anything. Goodbye, dear.'

She was standing by the drawing-room window, staring out into the garden, when Mrs Conroy came into the room to restore some of the newly burnished silver to its cabinet.

Her mother gave a little shriek. 'Good heavens, girl. I thought you'd gone up to change.'

'Oh, there's no hurry.' Amanda watched her fuss with the cabinet door, then said quietly, 'Mother—who was on the phone?'

Her mother fumbled the piece she was holding. 'Oh—just a message about the Parish Council meeting.'

'But that isn't for another fortnight, surely?'

'They're—trying to bring it forward.' Mrs Conroy was a poor liar, and she sounded flustered. 'Now, I must see to lunch.'

'I don't think I'm very hungry, after all. Perhaps I'll go for a drive.'

'No!' It was a squeal of anguish. 'You can't go out. You said you wouldn't.'

'I—suddenly feel like some fresh air.' Amanda looked steadily at her mother. 'And I think you know why. Tell me, who was really on the phone? It was Nigel, wasn't it?'

'Yes,' Mrs Conroy admitted wretchedly. 'It was. He rang yesterday—he'd found out somehow that you were coming down this weekend. He begged me to ask him here—to give him a last chance to win you back. He sounded so humble—so unhappy, Amanda, I couldn't bear it. No matter what the problem—however foolish you've been over his brother—I'm sure it can all be put right, if you just give Nigel a chance.'

'And you really won't believe that it's impossible.' Amanda gave a small, unhappy laugh. 'I'm sorry to spoil your plans, Mother, but I can't stay here under the circumstances.'

Mrs Conroy followed her, bleating, up the stairs. 'But what am I to tell him? What am I to say? He's expecting to see you—to find you here.'

'Tell him whatever seems best.' Amanda had hardly unpacked a thing from her case. It was as if she'd known, she thought ... She pushed down the lid, and clicked the locks. 'But don't be surprised if he loses his temper.'

'Where are you going?'

Amanda shrugged. 'Back to London, I suppose. What does it matter, anyway?' She saw her mother was crying, and planted a brief kiss on her cheek. 'Goodbye—I'll be in touch.'

But once she was in the car and on her way, she saw suddenly that her destination mattered very much indeed. If she went tamely back to the flat, then it would be the simplest thing in the world for Nigel to follow her there. And he would undeniably have Maggie and Fiona as allies, she realised with dismay.

Almost before she realised what she was doing, she had turned the car towards Aylesford Green. She didn't even know if Malory would be there, but perhaps she could persuade Mrs Priddy to let her take temporary refuge there while she considered her next move.

This time, as she pushed open the big white gates and walked up the drive, there was a welcoming bark and Harvey bounced to meet her, his tail wagging joyously. A second later, Malory followed him round the corner of the house.

When he saw her, he halted, his brows lifted en-quiringly. 'Amanda? This is an unexpected pleasure.'

'No, it isn't—not really.' She thrust her hands in the pockets of her coat to conceal the fact they were trembling. 'I—I had nowhere else to go, that's all.'

There was a silence, then he said equably, 'Fair enough. I'm glad you came here rather than the nearest pond.'

Amanda bit her lip. 'You'll never let me forget that madness, will you?'

'Eventually,' he said. 'You have to understand, it was one of the worst moments of my life, seeing you crawling up on to that parapet. I couldn't bear to think it was a member of my family who'd driven you to that sort of extremity.' He put a hand under her elbow. 'Come inside. It's starting to rain.'

She said inanely, 'Mother said it would,' and burst into tears. And that was the last thing she'd intended to do, she thought despairingly. She'd planned on being very calm, very matter of fact, very businesslike about her request for sanctuary.

She found herself in that lovely tranquil drawing-room, seated beside the fire, with Malory's handkerchief pressed to her face.

He said, 'I'll ask Mrs Priddy to bring some tea,' and she flung up a hand and caught at his sleeve.

'No—please. I don't want her—anyone—to see me making a fool of myself like this. I'll be all right in a minute.'

He nodded expressionlessly, and sat down op-posite her to wait. Harvey came and deposited an

NO COST! NO OBLIGATION TO BUY! NO PURCHASE NECESSARY!

PLAY "LUCKY 7" AND GET AS MANY AS SIX FREE GIFTS . . .

HOW TO PLAY:

1. With a coin, carefully scratch off the silver box at the right. This makes you eligible to receive one or more free books, and possibly other gifts, depending on what is revealed beneath the scatch-off area.

2. You'll receive brand-new Presents® novels. When you return this card, we'll send you the books and gifts you qualify for absolutely free!

3. Unless you tell us otherwise, every month we'll send you 8 additional novels to read and enjoy. If you decide to keep them, you'll pay only $1.99 per book*, a savings of 26¢ per book. There is no extra charge for postage and handling. There are no hidden extras.

4. When you join Harlequin Reader Service, we'll send you additional free gifts from time to time, as well as our newsletter.

5. You must be completely satisfied. You may cancel at any time just by dropping us a line or returning a shipment of books at our cost.

* Terms and prices subject to change.

HARLEQUIN "NO RISK" GUARANTEE

- You're not required to buy a single book—ever!
- You must be completely satisfied or you may return a shipment of books and cancel at any time.
- The free books and gifts you receive from this "Lucky 7" offer remain yours to keep in any case.

If offer card is missing, write to:
Harlequin Reader Service, 901 Fuhrmann Blvd., P.O. Box 1867, Buffalo, NY 14269-1867

DETACH AND MAIL CARD TODAY

anxious nose on her knee, whining a little, and she rubbed his head, smiling in spite of herself.

'He's so sweet.'

'Tell the postman that,' Malory said laconically. 'But first tell me what's happened.'

She concentrated her attention on Harvey's ears. 'I found Mother had invited Nigel over for a special lunch—a grand reconciliation. I couldn't face it, so I ran away.'

'There isn't,' he said slowly, 'a great deal he can do with your mother around. There was no real need to be afraid.'

'I wasn't afraid of him,' she said. She lifted her head, and met his gaze steadily. 'I was afraid of myself. Of giving way—of letting myself love him again—still.'

'You feel that's still a possibility?'

She said in a low voice, 'I know it is. And I think he knows it. That must be why he persists, mustn't it?'

'Either that, or he's fed up with playing the wronged and melancholy lover, and has decided to grab the initiative again as the romantic lead.'

She swallowed. 'Well, whatever it is, it made me realise that wherever I went he'd follow me—except here. So that's why I'm inflicting myself on you like this. I—I must apologise.'

'There's really no need,' he said. 'You're quite right, of course. This is the nearest thing to sanctuary you're likely to find.'

'And it won't be for very long,' she assured him. 'I'll see my boss—ask for a transfer to Brussels or Vienna.'

'Or anywhere,' Malory said ironically. 'And what if Nigel decided this is a victory he has to win, and follows you to your new locale? What then?'

She stared at him, her lips parting in horror. 'He couldn't—he wouldn't . . . Not abroad.'

'You don't think so?'

Amanda bent her head. 'It never even crossed my mind,' she said wretchedly.

'Then consider it now.' Malory got to his feet. 'And when I come back, I have a suggestion to put to you.' He gave her a brief, friendly smile and left the room.

Amanda sat staring dully at the leaping flames in the grate. She felt as if she'd reached the end of some weary road, to find all further progress blocked. It had never occurred to her that Nigel might be prepared to continue his pursuit of her indefinitely, but, when she considered his bizarre and egocentric behaviour in the past, she could find little difficulty in believing he might take a perverse pleasure in dogging her footsteps, even to another country. And she knew she would be unable to withstand that kind of insidious pressure. Yet the thought of reviving any kind of relationship with Nigel was frankly abhorrent.

Perhaps she could avoid him somehow—get an injunction—change her name. She made a little sound. It was Nigel who was in the wrong, and yet she had to become the fugitive.

She thought, 'What am I going to do?' and only realised she had spoken out loud when Malory said, from the doorway, 'Actually, there is a way—that is, if you genuinely want to be free of Nigel for ever.'

Amanda winced. 'Yes,' she said chokingly. 'Yes, I do.'

'Then it's quite simple,' he said. 'I get a special licence, and you marry me just as soon as it can be arranged.'

There was a profound silence. Amanda felt all the colour draining from her face as she stared at him.

Eventually, she said, 'That's impossible.'

'On the contrary.' Malory strolled across the room, and resumed his seat opposite her. 'Special licences can be obtained with relative ease.'

'I—I didn't mean that.' As he well knew, she thought, her pulses going crazy. 'Oh, I shouldn't have come here. I'll go.' As she tried to rise, he halted her with a gesture.

'Stop running, Amanda, and start thinking. What have you got against the idea?'

'Well, I should have thought that was obvious,' she said warmly. She spread her hands, palms upwards. 'A pretend engagement is bad enough, but marriage is something else again. I mean, you can't think that I—— You haven't considered all the implications.'

Malory's face was expressionless. 'Well, I certainly have no difficulty in considering the implication at the forefront of your mind,' he said coldly. 'Stop beating about the bush, Amanda. What you mean is, you don't want to sleep with me.'

Amanda stared down at her hands twisted together in her lap, praying he wouldn't make any edged remarks about her response to him the previous night. 'Well—yes,' she agreed in a stifled voice.

He sounded almost bored. 'Correct me if I'm wrong, but I have no recollection of ever asking you to go to bed with me. In fact,' he added, his mouth twisting, 'on the sole occasion we spent the night together, it was at your invitation.' He shrugged. 'So, what's the problem?'

Amanda was blushing all over. He didn't have to sound so—so bloody *dismissive* about it, she thought savagely. In spite of her mortification, she decided to try and retrieve the situation.

'But you must want a—a normal life,' she protested. She cast round wildly in her mind. 'Children, for example.'

Malory shrugged again. 'Perhaps I'm not very paternally minded,' he countered evenly. 'And I don't pass my life consumed by uncontrollable lust, either. You really have nothing to worry about, Amanda. I've never forced myself on any woman.' He leaned forward, making her look him in the eyes. 'I give you my solemn word that I won't make a move towards you without your express invitation.'

She said shakily, 'Then you're going to lead a very celibate life.'

'Not,' he said calmly, 'necessarily.'

She stared at him. 'You mean you'd find someone else?'

'That,' he said, 'is hardly any of your business, Amanda,' and she blushed again.

She was silent for a moment. Then, 'But you can't be marrying me for pure philanthropy,' she protested. 'Just to save me from Nigel.'

'By no means,' he said. 'I'm in dire need of a hostess—someone to help me with my business entertaining, particularly. Unfortunately, I have no convenient female relations I can call on.'

Amanda swallowed. 'Is that all?' she asked in a hollow voice.

Malory considered for a moment. 'Well, if you could exercise Harv for me, I'd be grateful. He doesn't always behave very well for Mrs Priddy, although she does her best with him.'

Amanda worked this out. 'You'd want me to give up my job?'

'I'd prefer it,' he said, 'but it isn't a condition.'

She said, 'This has to be the most bizarre proposal ever.'

The firm mouth relaxed into a faint smile. 'Probably.' He paused. 'Remember, Amanda, once you're my wife, you'll be safe from Nigel's manoeuvres.'

'Yĕs—— At least, I don't know.' She pressed her hands to her face. 'But we might make each other hideously unhappy as well.'

'It's possible. But if this non-marriage palls on either of us, we can always make other arrangements. After all, divorce has never been easier.'

'No,' she admitted in a small voice. She bit her lip. 'But this can't be the kind of relationship you ever visualised—ever wanted for yourself?'

'No. But when what you want is out of reach, it's sensible to settle for what you can get.'

How could he sound so matter of fact? she wondered, swallowing. He was turning both their lives upside-down, after all.

She jumped nervously as the drawing-room door opened and Mrs Priddy appeared with a tea tray.

'It's nice to see you here again, Miss Conroy.' She managed to invest the words with a faint reproof. 'George and I were both wondering when you'd be here for another visit.'

'She's here to stay this time, Mrs Priddy,' Malory said, before Amanda could open her mouth. He sent her a swift smile. 'We've decided to avoid any further publicity by being married very quietly next week, and Miss Conroy will be living here until the ceremony.' He turned to Amanda. 'When you've finished your tea, darling, go upstairs with Mrs Priddy and decide which bedroom you'd like.'

Mrs Priddy's face had become slightly tight-lipped, but at his final words a definite thaw set in. The housekeeper obviously shared Mrs Conroy's views on pre-marital sex, Amanda realised, torn between annoyance and amusement. She wondered what expression she would adopt when she realised her employer and his wife intended to continue using separate rooms after the ceremony as well.

'Very good, Dr Templeton. If Miss Conroy will give me her keys, I'll tell George to get her luggage from the car.'

'It's only one small case, actually,' Amanda mumbled, and Mrs Priddy gave her an indulgent look.

'Well, you'll have all the fun of choosing a new trousseau, won't you, madam?' She nodded at them both maternally. 'I'll just go and tell George the happy news.'

When she'd gone, Amanda said fierily, 'You do have a way of taking things into your own hands.'

'I needed to.' He poured a cup of tea and passed it to her. 'You looked like a girl suffering from a severe case of indecision, and it's quite unnecessary. You're here and you're safe. That's all that matters.'

She said in a subdued voice, 'I suppose so.'

But she was not convinced.

Amanda was even less convinced after the tour of the house which Mrs Priddy enthusiastically led her on later that day. Nigel would have supported her in comfort, she thought, but Malory was in a different league altogether, and the realisation disturbed her.

She hadn't simply acquired a shelter, but a luxurious nest. And she had no intention of sitting back and letting Malory support her, she decided, frowning. She was already getting by far the better side of this outrageous bargain. She wasn't going to be financially dependent on Malory as well.

'And this,' Mrs Priddy announced smilingly, throwing open yet another door, 'is the master bedroom.'

Amanda swallowed, glancing rather wildly at the large, modern four-poster bed which took pride of place. 'It's—lovely.'

'It has its own dressing-room—and bathroom,' Mrs Priddy demonstrated. She lowered her voice.

'But it's a bit stark for my taste, madam. The décor needs a feminine touch.'

Out of the corner of her eye, Amanda saw that Malory had joined them. 'I—I wouldn't change a thing,' she said, crossly aware that she was blushing again, to Mrs Priddy's overt approval.

'You can change anything but the bed, darling.' To her fury, Malory draped a casual arm across her shoulders. 'It was made in the village by the local carpenter—the last commission he accepted before his retirement. He designed all the carvings himself,' he went on, sending her a wicked grin. 'I understand most of them are fertility symbols.'

'Indeed they're not!' Mrs Priddy said severely. 'So stop teasing the young lady, Mr Malory, do.'

'Not another word,' Malory promised. He smiled at Amanda. 'Have you chosen your own bedroom yet, my sweet?'

'Yes,' she said hastily. She glanced at Mrs Priddy. 'Was it the west room, did you say, Mrs Priddy?'

'Very suitable,' Malory said, so silkily that she knew he'd guessed she'd chosen it because it was the furthest from his own room.

But that wasn't the only reason, she thought rebelliously. She'd fallen for the tiny green-flowered print which covered the walls and supplied the fabric for the furnishings, and the light, elegant, furniture. It was a charming room, and it needed to be, considering the amount of time she'd be spending there!

She became aware that Mrs Priddy had tactfully made herself scarce, and shook off his arm. 'Please don't do that.'

'Just a moment.' He wasn't teasing any more, or even faintly amused. 'Let me make one thing clear. Whatever our private differences, in public the act goes on.'

She bit her lip. 'I'm sorry. I suppose I'm over-reacting, but the circumstances aren't exactly—usual.'

'You'll learn to adapt to them, I'm sure. I suggest that, as soon as we're married, we do the conventional thing and go on a honeymoon.' His tone was curt. 'I was planning to take a holiday, anyway. Have you any preference as to destination?'

She moistened her dry lips with the tip of her tongue. 'If you really think it's necessary, I'll leave the choice to you.'

He nodded. 'We'll have to do something about your passport, of course.'

'My current one's at the flat.' There was a feeling of total unreality about the entire conversation, Amanda thought weakly. She couldn't be standing discussing travel arrangements for her own honeymoon with Malory Templeton, this comparative stranger she was pledged to marry.

He must have sensed her inner confusion, because he said gently, 'Leave the details to me. Why don't you go and unpack and rest before dinner?'

'Thank you,' she muttered. She sent him an awkward look. 'This is an awful lot of trouble to go to just to find yourself a hostess.'

'Ah, but that isn't all I hope to gain,' he said.

She was tense suddenly. Was he warning her already that he intended to bend the rules of their agreement? she wondered.

She said huskily, 'What else is there?'

He put a finger under her chin, tilting her face up towards him. He said softly, 'As I told you last night, darling, the pleasure of your company—and the promise of future delight.'

He let her go, and walked away downstairs, leaving her staring after him. She went to her room, closed the door, locked it, and lay down on the bed.

She had come here for sanctuary, she thought. And Malory had told her she was safe. So, why was it she had never felt more insecure in her life?

CHAPTER SEVEN

AMANDA walked along the warm edge of the sea, small waves foaming delicately round her ankles.

This was her favourite time of day, she thought, these moments before sunset, and the swift, almost magical descent of the tropical Balinese night. And it was a time when she was certain of having the beach to herself.

Already, twinkling lights were beginning to appear in the lush vegetation of the rambling hotel gardens. When they'd arrived three weeks before, she'd been exhausted, both by the flight and by the emotional pressures of the preceding days, and she'd thought dazedly, as a pair of white-coated porters led them down winding paths, past waterfalls and tiny lakes afloat with lilies, that she'd stumbled into paradise.

It was an impression which had lingered. The hotel complex had tucked its luxurious bungalows in the heart of its gardens, creating for each of them an illusion of privacy and isolation.

Under ordinary circumstances, Amanda could imagine no more magical place for a honeymoon. But the circumstances were far from ordinary, and the magic had been confined firmly to their surroundings.

Amanda gave a small, wry smile. The fact that Malory had chosen to start their pretend marriage in such a romantic spot had aroused, initially, all her worst misgivings. And these had been compounded when she saw the immense double bed which dominated the room in which their luggage had been placed. She'd stood, staring at it with blank eyes, while Malory thanked the porters and tipped them.

When they were alone, he'd said, drily, 'Don't look so stricken, darling. There's another room across the hall.' And he'd removed his bags there without further delay.

It had been, she had to admit, the only awkward moment she had experienced, and that was largely due to Malory's completely prosaic attitude to their situation.

Once she had been able to accept the fact that he had meant what he said, and she wasn't going to have to fight him off each night, Amanda had begun to relax, and even to enjoy herself.

She had flung herself headlong into an orgy of trips and sightseeing, with his amused encouragement. But Malory himself did not accompany her. This was not, he'd told her pleasantly, his first trip to Bali.

She'd been slightly disconcerted by this, without really knowing why. She'd found herself asking, 'Did you come here alone?'

'No.' There had been a note in his voice which definitely discouraged further questions, but she supposed his companion had been female. And she no longer found that as extraordinary as she would have done at the start of their relationship.

Although he had never referred to it, Amanda still felt hot with embarrassment when she recalled her shaming response to his lovemaking. And it had occurred to her with annoying frequency that Malory might be altogether a more skilful and sophisticated lover than she'd given him credit for.

But the only certainty was that he had no apparent wish to make love to her. Indeed, his attitude throughout had been almost that of tolerant older brother with indulged younger sister. For instance, he'd encouraged her to spend a small fortune on the exquisite silverwork and woodcarving for which Bali was famous, including presents for the Priddys, and for Mrs Conroy.

Amanda had hesitated over the latter, the memory of her mother's hysterical reaction to the news of her forthcoming marriage still only too fresh in her mind. Mrs Conroy had at first refused point-blank to come to the register office ceremony, and then had performed a suspiciously hasty U-turn, demanding exact details of where and when the wedding was going to take place.

So that she can tell Nigel, no doubt, Amanda had realised wearily, and replaced the telephone receiver with a quiet, 'Goodbye, Mother.'

She could only hope that, now she was actually Malory's wife, Mrs Conroy would abandon her attempts to bring about a reconciliation between Nigel and herself. And that Nigel, too, would finally admit defeat, and keep out of her life, she thought, a little knot of wretchedness lodging itself in the region of her breastbone. However determinedly she might fill her days, there were still the nights to get through, when she lay staring into the darkness, her mind filled with an odd restlessness.

Amanda looked at the sky, its serenity pierced and transformed by the setting sun into a richness of purple and crimson shot with gold. All the colours, she thought with a little sigh, of the exquisite, filmy sarong she was wearing over her bikini.

It was the most exotic thing she'd ever possessed, and she would never have dreamed of buying such a thing for herself, only Malory had insisted. It had been entirely his own choice, and the nearest to a romantic gesture he'd made during their whole stay.

For which she could only be grateful, she told herself resolutely. Because, in spite of his forbearance, his care to leave her to her own devices as much as possible, she had been aware, when she was with him, of little pangs of yearning and regret which had a danger all their own. It was the atmosphere of the place getting to her, she thought. Brilliant sunlit days, and sultry moonlit nights were bound to have an effect eventually, and perhaps it was just as well they were flying back tomorrow.

She felt a small frisson of awareness, and, glancing back towards the gardens which bordered the beach, saw Malory standing under a tree, watching her.

She lifted a hand rather uncertainly in greeting, and he began to walk over the pale sand towards her. He'd never disturbed her at this special time before. Usually, when she got back to the bungalow to change for dinner, he was sitting on the small veranda, reading or enjoying a reflective drink. It was the first time he'd sought her out like this.

'Is something wrong?' She came out of the water.

'Not a thing.' Malory smiled at her. 'It seems a dance troupe are going to perform the Ramayana ballet after dinner tonight, and I wondered if you'd like to see it. If not, we could always eat somewhere else.'

'Oh, no, I'd love it.' Amanda had found herself entranced by the colour and artistry of the Balinese myths and legends portrayed in their dances. 'Will it be those gorgeous children again, I wonder?' She paused. 'But, of course, you've seen it all before. We don't have to...'

'I didn't realise I was such a killjoy,' Malory cut rather drily across her stilted words.

'You're not,' Amanda protested swiftly. 'But you didn't want to see any of the temples, or the craft villages...'

'Because I didn't want to inflict my undiluted company on you all day and every day,' he said without rancour.

'Oh—heavens,' Amanda stammered. 'I—I hope you haven't been too bored.'

'Certainly not,' he said. 'It's been a hell of year, and I've enjoyed the chance to relax.' He sounded maddeningly matter of fact.

Her shrug tried to match his tone. 'That's what holidays are for.' The movement of her shoulders made her sarong slip a little, and she clutched at it with unwarranted haste. Surely she'd got over feeling self-conscious about appearing before Malory in her bikini by now, she castigated herself, as she retied the knot, aware that he was watching her hurried movements with a faint smile.

She began to babble. 'I came down to watch my last sunset.' She gestured to where the sky was beginning to deepen to indigo. 'Isn't that the most beautiful thing you've ever seen?'

'Yes.'

There was an odd note in the quiet voice, and she glanced at him to discover, with shock, that he wasn't looking at the sunset at all, but at her. And he wasn't smiling, either. There was a kind of brooding stillness in his face that started her heart knocking unevenly against her ribcage. Even in the bungalow at night, she realised confusedly, they had never seemed so—alone as they were now.

She stepped backwards, stumbling a little in the soft sand. Her voice shook as she said, 'I'd better go and change for dinner.'

'It might be best,' he agreed expressionlessly. 'I'll see you later.'

She had to overcome a strong urge to run away from him up the beach. As she wrestled her sandals on to her sandy feet, she told herself she was being ridiculous. Malory was entitled to look at her if he wanted to. He'd paid, after all, for every stitch she was wearing. And her bikini, though brief, was quite decent. None of which explained why she'd felt so vulnerable—and naked, suddenly.

For the first time, that evening, she fastened the bolt on the bathroom door before taking her shower.

She'd brought the golden culotte dress with her, and had intended to wear it that evening, but after a moment's irresolution she thrust it back in the wardrobe. It held too many connotations, she told herself defensively as she closed the zip on a pretty jade-green dress with a wide scooped neckline and wrap-around skirt.

The Ramayana was as spectacular as she could have wished, its theme the conflict between good and evil, as so many Balinese ballets depicted. Amanda was intrigued to see that the roles of the two princely brothers, sent by intrigue into exile, were danced by women, Rama in a golden crown and Laksmana in a black one. She was completely carried away by the story of kidnapping, demons and enchantment which followed, with Rama's wife, Sita, being snatched away by the evil tyrant Rawana in his hideous mask.

She loved the animals, too, which were such a feature of the performance—the golden deer which lured Rama away from his wife, and the heroic Jatayu bird which tried to rescue her from her captor, not to mention the monkeys whose caperings added a touch of broad slapstick to the performance.

As the Monkey God, Hanumen, led Sita to rejoin her husband in triumph at the end, Amanda clapped until her hands tingled.

'I'll never forget it—never,' she told Malory ecstatically. 'Oh, this is the most wonderful place in the world. If only...' She stopped dead.

'Yes?' Malory prompted gently enough, but with a closed expression in his face.

'Nothing,' she said, with a little unhappy gasp.

'Let me guess,' he said harshly. 'If only you could have been here with the man you love. Isn't that it?'

Amanda flushed dully, 'I suppose so.' She lifted her chin with a touch of defiance. 'What else do you expect?'

There was a brief, loaded silence, then he lifted his shoulders in a shrug. 'Not a thing.' His smile did not reach his eyes, as he extended a formal hand to her. 'Shall we go and sample the delights of the *Ristafel*?'

'What's that?' Amanda tried to restore the easy footing of the past few weeks, which her tactless slip of the tongue had endangered.

'A Dutch rice table,' he said. 'An Indonesian buffet with more dishes than you can dream of.' His mouth twisted satirically. 'Another memory for you to cherish.'

She followed him miserably. It had all turned sour, suddenly, and she couldn't understand why it had happened. Those two small words had made it sound as if she'd been longing and grieving for Nigel all the time, and that wasn't true at all. Perhaps hearts didn't break as easily as she'd thought, or maybe she was just totally disillusioned with his egocentric, vicious behaviour.

People were already clustering around the long tables, exclaiming happily over the food. There were few families at the hotel, she noticed. Most of the guests were couples, and she was sure that she and Malory were not the only honeymooners. She found herself noticing with a kind of heightened consciousness the linked hands, the exchanged smiles and intimate, lingering looks that spoke of fulfilled love.

The food looked wonderful—Amanda saw her favourite *nasi goreng* and duck broiled in a banana leaf among the dishes—but she wasn't hungry any more.

She touched Malory's sleeve. 'I—I think I'll go back to the bungalow.' She saw him begin to frown, and went on hurriedly, 'We have a long flight ahead of us, and I'm rather tired.'

'Just as you wish,' he said after a pause. 'Do you want me to walk you back?'

She forced a smile. 'Why—because the demon king, Rawana, might be waiting to snatch me away? No, I'll be fine. Enjoy your dinner.'

She slipped away through the throng. She would occupy herself with some packing, she thought, and save time in the morning.

But when she was by herself, she found she was in no real hurry to return to the bungalow. A sliver of moon had appeared above the trees, and she lingered on one of the fragile-seeming bridges, looking at its reflection in the pool beneath.

She had once read somewhere that if you captured the moon in the water, your wish would be granted, and found she was wondering what she would wish for, if it was true.

But she knew what she wanted. She wished for the past weeks to be wiped away, and Nigel to be waiting for her at Calthorpe, loving and faithful.

The reflection blurred and fragmented as a fish broke the surface of the pool, and she was glad, because—just for a moment—she'd seen another, very different, image in the water.

And that made no sense at all, because Malory was the last person in the world she wanted—wasn't he?

Wasn't he? she appealed to that cold, ironic little moon, then turned away, thankful that she was alone. Because, if Malory had been with her, she knew that, on this island for lovers, she would have been tempted to go into his arms.

And that, of course, was impossible even to contemplate.

Could there be a damper, bleaker month than January? Amanda asked herself in exasperation as she marched across the soggy field in Harvey's eager wake. And could there be a worse day to spend on one's own than Sunday?

Although, of course, she wasn't entirely alone, she amended. The Priddys were there, and she had Harvey, who was currently investigating a ditch with the enthusiasm of a dog who has just discovered some particularly noisome unpleasantness.

She called him to heel and he came, looking so consciously virtuous that Amanda forgot to be grumpy, and burst out laughing. 'You fraud,' she told him, rubbing the top of his head. 'As soon as your master gets back from his trip, you know quite well you'll give me the elbow.'

She had spent a considerable part of the past six weeks waiting for Malory to return from some journey or another. She'd told herself it was only to be expected, then heard Mrs Priddy declare one

day to George that she'd never known Dr
Templeton spend so much time away from home
before.

Amanda whisked herself out of earshot before
the good woman was tempted to speculate on the
cause. It was naturally never referred to, but
Amanda knew the housekeeper was still reeling
from the separate bedrooms issue.

She sighed as she unhitched the gate that led into
the lane. Life had been far from easy since she had
returned from their honeymoon. She'd decided to
leave work, or perhaps it was fairer to say work
had decided to leave her, since she'd discovered, on
presenting herself back at the office, that her suc-
cessor was being briskly trained. Jeffrey had been
frankly and brutally chauvinistic about his reasons.
'I want a girl who can keep her mind on her job,
not a dewy-eyed bride planning the evening dinner
for two,' he'd told her. 'But there's a spot in per-
sonnel you can have until you get pregnant.'

She had thanked him quietly, and handed in her
notice. She'd observed in the past that Jeffrey never
had married women working in his department, but
it had never occurred to her that his prejudice could
apply to her. One of these days, she thought, he
would end up in front of an industrial tribunal.

And now she had to adapt herself to the slower
pace of life at Aylesford Green. She had discovered
almost at once that Malory had been telling no less
than the truth when he'd said he needed a hostess.
There had been a number of drinks parties and
dinners over the Christmas period, and she felt
she'd handled them with aplomb. Certainly, he'd

ventured no criticism. Well, at least she could play that particular role for him, she thought with a little sigh. And it seemed to be all he wanted from her. She closed the gate, and let Harvey run ahead of her, along the verge towards the house.

The realisation that Malory might be deliberately avoiding her had been a disturbing one. She had found herself wondering more than once if he'd decided their hasty marriage had been a fatal mistake, and whether his frequent absences were a hint that he was planning to end it as soon as decently possible. But what was a suitable time-span for a marriage which had never really begun? Amanda asked herself restlessly.

To her bewilderment, she had discovered that the house seemed barely alive when Malory was away. Not that he sought her company particularly when he did come home, she reminded herself wryly. And, when they *were* together, he was polite, but aloof.

She'd been amazed, too, to find that when he was expected back she was on edge, watching the windows, listening for the sound of his car. She made sure also that Mrs Priddy had cooked something he particularly liked for dinner, and found herself taking extra trouble with her clothes and make-up. Not, she thought, that he ever seemed to notice. The last time he had looked at her—really looked—had been that evening on the beach in Bali. Maybe she should turn up the central heating, and greet him in her bikini and sarong, Amanda suggested to herself, digging her hands into the pockets of her sheepskin coat.

Or maybe she should remember why they had got married in the first place, and stop trying to attract his attention in any degree. After all, what did it matter whether he noticed her, or what he thought about her? She'd wanted a refuge from Nigel, and he'd wanted a hostess, so they should both be perfectly satisfied.

But I'm not a bit content, she thought morosely. And I'm not sleeping properly, either. You could store potatoes in the bags under my eyes. And it's always worse when he's away, because I can't stop remembering what he said about not staying celibate and—imagining things.

She rounded the last bend before the house, and stopped with a groan. Harvey was sitting on the verge, whimpering, one paw held pathetically in the air.

'Oh, Harv!' She crouched beside him. 'What have you done to yourself?' She took the paw, and tried to examine it. There was no obvious wound, but she didn't know what to look for, and Harvey, as if sensing her uncertainty, yelped, then growled softly.

'I can't carry you—you're too heavy,' she told him, straightening. She walked slowly, and he limped beside her through the gate on to the drive.

And there, in front of the house, was Malory's car. Amanda stopped short, aware that she had flushed suddenly, and that her heart seemed to be beating twice as fast as normal.

It was shock, she told herself defensively. After all, he hadn't been expected back until tomorrow.

At that moment, Malory appeared in the doorway. He was still in the dark formality of his business clothes, and he looked tired, Amanda thought, breaking into a little run.

She said breathlessly, 'Malory—I'm so glad you're home!'

His brows lifted, and he managed a shadow of a grin. 'I'm deeply flattered. What's brought this about?'

'It's Harvey,' she said. 'He's got something wrong with his paw. Will you have a look, or shall I call the vet?'

His smile faded. 'I'll see to him.' He squatted on his haunches, persuading the spaniel, without difficulty, to roll over on his back. Amanda joined them, kneeling on the damp gravel.

She watched the long deft fingers probing gently in a way she wouldn't have dared emulate. Malory talked to the dog softly, his blue eyes intent as he bent over him.

He needed a shave, Amanda thought, her own gaze fixed almost obsessively on his face. There was a shadow of stubble along his jawline. She found herself wanting to rub her fingers along the faint roughness of his skin and smooth away the lines of tension beside his mouth. It was a very long time since the one and only occasion he'd kissed her, but she could remember how his lips had felt on her own, and the totally male scent of his skin. She could breathe it now, she thought wonderingly, or was it her mind playing tricks?

He said with quiet triumph, 'There,' and showed her the long thorn he'd just extracted from Harvey's pad.

'I couldn't see a thing.' She was glad that bending over the dog gave her an excuse for her hectically heightened colour.

'He often picks things up like that,' he said. 'And he's a terrible hypochondriac. I bet he limps for a week.' He rose lithely. 'And he seems to have been rolling in something iffy, too. Maybe you could sweet-talk George into giving him a bath, while I get out of this damned suit.' He gave her a swift, perfunctory smile and went into the house.

Amanda watched him go, then walked Harvey round to the back door, where George cheerfully took charge of him.

She tugged off her muddy boots and left them next to the cupboard in the rear passage. She made herself move slowly and deliberately, feeling every pulse-beat echo through her being like the slam of a sledge hammer. She could think of nothing but the weariness in Malory's face and the way his smile had died when he realised her welcome had strings.

Her stockinged feet made no sound on the stairs, nor along the carpeted landing.

His bedroom door was open, but the room seemed deserted. For a moment, she was frozen with disappointment, then he came out of the bathroom, drying his hands on a towel. He'd discarded his jacket, waistcoat and tie, and his hair was ruffled. He stopped when he saw her, his brows lifting in surprise.

'More problems?' he asked with a kind of resignation. 'Won't they keep?'

She shook her head. She supposed she should say something, but no words would come—at least, none that meant anything.

She went to him, standing on tiptoe to slide her arms round his neck, drawing down his head so she could kiss his unsmiling mouth.

He was so still, he could have been carved from rock, and for one terrible minute she thought he was going to reject her. Then his arms went fiercely round her, pulling her against him so roughly that her body felt jarred, and he was kissing her, his mouth parting hers to receive the urgent thrust of his tongue.

Amanda was trembling under the onslaught, but she was exhilarated, too. That iron guard of his was down, and he was holding her as if he could not get her close enough, his lips searching hers, extracting every last sweet secret. His hand twisted in her chestnut hair, pulling her head back so he could kiss her throat above the collar of her cashmere sweater. A sound escaped her, half startled, half excited, as his other hand cupped her breast through the fine wool, his fingers teasing her hardening nipple.

Amanda felt herself sway in his arms, deaf to everything but the clamour in her blood, and slowly he lifted his head, and held her for a moment, steadied against him.

He took her unresisting hand, stroked the soft palm with the tip of his forefinger, then dropped a kiss on to her wrist before walking with her to the door.

She was choked with bewilderment, and then she realised he was only closing the door, and turning the key gently but definitely in the lock. Shutting them in together.

He led her over to the bed, then slowly, almost reverently, he began to free the buttons which closed the front of her sweater.

At once, her hands came up to stop him. No matter how much she had invited this, there was no way she could stand there in broad daylight and let Malory undress her.

She said, stammering a little. 'I—I can manage.'

The blue eyes studied her quizzically for a moment, then he bent and kissed her swiftly on the mouth before walking round to the other side of the bed. Turning his back on her, he began to remove his own clothing.

Amanda turned the other way, too. It was ridiculous, she knew, considering the way she had thrown herself at him, but she'd never been naked with a man before, and she felt shy.

She tumbled out of her clothes, dropping them on to the floor, and scrambled into bed, pulling the covers up to her chin. The linen sheets felt faintly chilly, and she shivered.

The mattress shifted slightly as he joined her, and she shivered again, lying on her side, staring sightlessly across the room, suddenly, shatteringly aware of his naked, starkly aroused body lying next to hers.

Malory's hands were warm on her bare shoulders as he turned her inexorably to face him.

He said quietly, 'Are you sure this is what you want?'

She wasn't sure about anything. The warm tide of feeling which had swept her here into his arms—his bed—was ebbing fast, leaving a kind of sick panic in its wake. But she couldn't draw back now, because she knew she would never have the courage to offer herself again. She lifted a hand and stroked his dark hair, and drew him down to her, letting the action speak for her.

He kissed her slowly, softly, his mouth exploring hers as if there was all the time in the world, and he intended to use every minute of it. Then he pulled the covers away from her shoulders, making it clear that he was going to look as well as touch. Her body seemed to quiver under his gaze, and she had to clamp her jaws together to stop her teeth from chattering.

He touched her breasts as if they were flowers he was afraid to crush, then bent to adore their proud rosy buds with his lips. She caught her breath at the sharp delight of the sensation, and felt him smile against her skin. His hands stroked the length of her body, finding pulses, nerve-endings, secret responses she had never dreamed existed. She felt dazedly as if she were some deep and private mystery to which he alone had the key.

But she was thankful he did not seem to demand any reciprocal caresses from her.

As Malory's hand feathered over the curve of her hip, and drifted down to part her thighs, she tensed, and he whispered, 'It's all right, darling, just relax.'

But that was easier said than done. This was entirely new to her, this slow, lingering exploration of her most intimate self, and her body's greedy reaction to his touch terrified her. She didn't want to feel like this—as if she had no will of her own, no existence beyond the caress of those all too knowing fingers. She didn't want this sense of helplessness, as if she was being carried along on a current too strong for her to fight.

She wanted the mystery solved. She reached for him, her untutored hands fumbling, trying to learn from his response what he wanted from her, her mind shrinking, at the same time, from the strength and power of his maleness and all that it implied.

He said, 'Oh, Christ,' the words torn from his throat. Then, 'Amanda—no——I can't . . .'

He pushed her back against the pillows, and his body covered hers with a swift urgency that transcended all else. His face was a stranger's, suddenly stripped of all emotion except desire, the blue eyes glittering. Like ice, she thought, ice that burned . . .

She cried out, first in fear, then in pain, and the pain filled her mind, and her body. As her muscles tautened against the shock of his invasion of her flesh, she felt as if she was being torn apart, and she pushed unavailingly at his shoulders.

'Stop it! Leave me alone!'

He said again, 'I can't . . .' and it was like a cry of despair.

She lay beneath him, crushed and outraged, her body rigid with resentment. It didn't even matter that the pain had stopped. She had given herself to him, trusted him, and he had betrayed her.

He groaned as his body reached its goal and shuddered against hers. She felt bruised, not merely by his physical possession of her, but by her own anger and disappointment. She lay silent and unmoving, until at last he rolled away from her, and lay, his face buried in the pillow, his breathing harsh and uneven.

She took a breath of her own. In a small voice, icy with distaste, she said, 'Is that—*that*—what all the fuss is about?'

Malory lifted himself on to one elbow, and looked down at her, his face guarded. He said, 'Not exactly...'

'I'm delighted to hear it,' she said. 'Otherwise, the human race would have died out centuries ago.'

There was a pause, then he said quietly, 'I know it's no excuse, but when you touched me like that, my control just—snapped...'

'Oh, I see,' she said. 'Then it's all my fault.'

'It's not a question of fault—although I should have realised earlier from your reaction how totally innocent you were.' He touched her face gently with his hand. 'Darling, I did try to warn you that there's no such thing as instant bliss.'

'So you did,' she said, bitterly sarcastic. 'What a fool I was not to heed your warning.' She turned her head away, rejecting his touch.

His mouth hardened. He said, too evenly, 'I'm sorry the earth didn't move for you, my sweet. Perhaps you'll be more lucky next time.'

He threw back the covers and got out of bed, reaching down to pick up his discarded clothes from the floor.

She said in a low, shaking voice, 'There isn't going to be any next time.'

For a moment, he stood in silence, then he took the covers she was holding defensively, and ripped them from her clutch. Ashamed and angry, she cried out, trying to shield herself with her hands while his glance raked mercilessly down her naked body.

He said softly, almost menacingly, 'Oh, yes, there bloody well is.' He tossed the sheet back over her, and walked away into the bathroom, slamming the door behind him.

She lay, watching the closed door with a kind of shocked disbelief, then slowly her stunned body began to tremble.

CHAPTER EIGHT

THE rain dashed itself against the window as if it was trying to break into the house, and Amanda shuddered, trying to punch the sofa cushions into a more comfortable shape. The desolation of the weather matched her own mood perfectly.

I must have been insane, she thought wretchedly. Completely and utterly mad. And now I've ruined everything.

She had fled to the sanctuary of her own room, locking herself in just in case Malory felt inclined to justify his threat by following her there, and inflicting himself on her again. But she'd been left strictly undisturbed, and had curled up into a miserable ball on her bed, crying until she had no more tears left. And when the storm of weeping had ended and she was calm again, she'd found she was able to think more clearly about what had happened.

There was no doubt that the whole episode had been an unmitigated disaster from every point of view, but she was no longer so inclined to heap all the blame for that on Malory.

She had never joined in the girl-talk confidences about sex at the flat, partly because she had felt that her love for Nigel was too precious and sacrosanct, but mainly because she'd had nothing to contribute but the depth of her own ignorance. Yet she hadn't been able to avoid overhearing some of the exchanges, and she could remember hearing Maggie or Fiona relating some horror story about her own 'first time' and how it had 'hurt like hell'.

Amanda recalled thinking smugly how different it would be for Nigel and herself. And so it might have been, she told herself defensively, with love to smooth the way.

But she didn't love Malory, and he didn't care for her, although she supposed that for him, and any man, a transient physical attraction was enough, and she knew he found her beautiful because he'd said so.

Amanda groaned. It had been total folly to fling herself at him like that, and she still couldn't fully understand how or why it had happened. I suppose it seemed like a good idea at the time, she thought wretchedly.

But that wasn't sufficient reason to turn the terms of their marriage upside down. In some paradoxical way, it was probably Malory's cool acceptance of those terms, his ability to distance himself, which had sparked off the powerful, inexplicable attraction which had built in her over the past weeks.

They say absence makes the heart grow fonder, she told herself, but her heart hadn't been involved—merely her hormones. And she'd discovered too late that that wasn't sufficient, and never could be. Which was why Malory had to be made to understand that this afternoon had been an aberration, not to be repeated.

He was a civilised man, she thought feverishly. She believed what he'd said about never forcing himself on a woman. But perhaps no other woman had made him quite as angry as she'd done.

She had a bath, and put on a simple black crêpe dress with a gold chain belt before going down-stairs. Her mirror told her that, although pale, she looked much as usual. There were no outer signs of the trauma she'd gone through.

Except I no longer have virginal eyes, she thought wryly.

But the calm, rational confrontation she'd en-visaged was not to be. A ruffled Mrs Priddy told her that Dr Templeton had gone out, giving no in-dication when he intended to return.

Amanda picked at a solitary dinner, then retired to the drawing-room to drink her way through a pot of black coffee.

She cast a glance at the carriage clock. It was getting incredibly late. Mrs Priddy had been in to clear the coffee away, and wish her goodnight. She supposed she should go to bed, but she wanted to see Malory and make some kind of peace with him first. Now, it occured to her for the first time that he might not be coming home that night.

Even as her mind recoiled from the implications of that, the door opened, and he walked in.

Dry-mouthed, she said, 'Hello. You—you've missed dinner...'

'I've eaten, thank you.' He sat down on the sofa opposite.

'Oh. Well, would you like a cup of coffee—or a drink?' She sounded like a hostess with an awkward guest, she thought with a pang.

He said politely, after a pause, 'A whisky, perhaps,' adding drily, 'The usual anodyne.'

She poured it for him, her hand shaking a little. She wished she'd been able to face him hours ago. As it was, she'd had the entire evening for her nervousness and embarrassment to build up.

She handed him his drink, and resumed her seat. Jerkily, she said, 'Malory, about this afternoon—I'm sorry.'

'So am I,' he said coolly. 'Let's consider the matter closed, shall we?'

'But we can't,' Amanda protested. 'I said some awful things to you.'

'I'll survive.'

'Yes, but—I shouldn't have criticised you—in that way...'

He smiled without humour. 'Advice to young wives?' he enquired ironically. 'Always praise your husband's performance in bed, however inept it may be? What agony column did that gem come from?'

She flushed. Nothing about this conversation was going as she intended. 'It didn't. But I want you to know I'm deeply ashamed about—everything. It should never have happened.'

He drank some of the whisky. 'As a matter of interest, why did it happen?'

'I—I don't understand...'

He sighed shortly. 'Yes, you do, Amanda. Why did you come to me as you did—offer yourself?'

She bent her head. 'I don't know,' she admitted in a muffled voice. 'I suppose I just wanted to know...'

'What sex was like?' He sounded faintly amused. 'Well, I'm glad I was able to satisfy your curiosity, if nothing else.'

She moved her shoulders uncomfortably. 'Don't. It—it wasn't your fault.'

'I've no intention of evading my share of the blame.' His voice was almost bored. 'I know quite well you weren't sufficiently aroused.' He shrugged. 'I was an impatient idiot.' He paused. 'Of course, if I'd had the least idea I was going to be seduced, I'd have contrived to come back from the conference slightly less tired and on edge.'

She swallowed. 'Why did you come back so early?'

'The last speaker went down with some twenty-four-hour virus and cancelled.'

'Oh.' She assimilated that, wondering what she'd been expecting him to say. That he'd been missing her so desperately, he couldn't stay away for a moment longer? Fat chance, under the circumstances, she thought in self-derision. 'Was—was it an interesting conference?'

'No.' He drank the remainder of the whisky and put down the tumbler. There was a purposefulness about the movement which alarmed her.

She said quickly, 'Well, if I can't get you any supper, I think I'll go up...'

'Not yet,' he said evenly. 'Come here, Amanda.' He patted the cushion beside him.

A muscle worked convulsively in her throat. 'I—
I don't want...'

'But I do.' His eyes met her pleading gaze, held
it. 'Don't make me fetch you.'

He spoke gently enough, but she didn't argue any
more. Mutely, she crossed the space between them,
and sat down beside him.

There was a silence, then he said, 'When I said
we should forget this afternoon, it was a nonsense.
We can't, of course.' He put out a hand and pushed
a strand of her hair behind her ear. His fingers caressed her lobe, and found the sensitive area underneath. In spite of herself, her throat arched in
shocked response.

But if she'd feared he would see that as a signal
to throw her on to the rug and jump on her, she
couldn't have been more wrong. The stroking hand
moved to the nape of her neck, sending small, delicious shivers rippling over her scalp. She was
almost purring by the time his fingers found the
metal tab of the zip at the back of her dress, and
began to propel it downwards.

The lazy brush of his fingers down her spine was
another undreamed of delight. Her shoulders
moved voluptuously, relishing each tiny sensation,
even while some appalled voice in her brain was
crying out that she couldn't be allowing this—she
couldn't...

He had unclipped the hook of her bra, and as
he pushed he dress off her shoulders, the under-
garment went with it, baring her to the waist. Her
small breasts felt oddly swollen, the nipples erect,
already eager for the touch of his hands—his lips.

His fingers shaped the soft, scented mounds, tugging gently at the tumescent peaks until a small moan shuddered out of her.

He lifted her then, so that she was lying across his thighs, in his arms, her cheek pressed against the soft kid of the casual jacket he was wearing. His hand slid up the cord in her neck and traced her jawline before cupping her face, turning it upwards for his kiss.

His lips barely touched hers, teasing her with a contact that was hardly more than a breath. His tongue flickered sensually along her lower lip, and she gasped, her head falling back against his shoulder in silent entreaty.

His fingers were warm on her knee under the demure black skirt, and she trembled as they slid upwards, over the stockinged smoothness, to the bare flesh of her thigh. Some hazy memory reminded her he'd once said he liked stockings, and he smiled into her eyes as if he'd remembered it, too.

Then, as his hand reclaimed her intimately, he bent his head, and his mouth possessed hers, deeply and passionately, preventing any protest she might have made.

Her body had tautened instinctively, because this was where it had all gone wrong before, yet she already knew that this time was different. Under the sensual sureness of his touch, she was melting, prey to needs she hadn't known existed until that moment.

His fingers stroked her, circled on her, leading her inexorably down some unknown path. She ached with something more than pain, her breasts almost violently tender, a faint film of sweat bedewing her forehead.

Her senses seemed to have a separate existence. Under his dictation, they swelled to a crescendo of feeling, then subsided over and over again, each time taking her fractionally nearer some mysterious summit of sensation.

Deep, deep within her, she felt something unfurling, like a flower opening its petals to the sun, so tenuous at first, she hardly dared acknowledge its existence, in case it escaped her.

As if he guessed, Malory's caress deepened, took on a more rhythmic intensity, and his mouth closed almost fiercely on her breast.

She heard a voice she hardly recognised as her own sob, 'Oh, God—please—please——' as the rhythm inside her suddenly became a frenzy, her body convulsing in an endless series of sharp, soaring pulsations, at the height of which she thought she would faint—or die.

The downward spiral back to sanity was slow, almost dreamy. She pressed her damp face into the breast of Malory's shirt, feeling totally spent, deliciously, wantonly lethargic.

All she wanted in this world was for Malory to lift her into his arms, and carry her upstairs to his bed. That deep primal throbbing still seemed to echo through her blood and bones, hinting at more pleasure to come. When, eventually, he moved, her nails curled into his shoulders like a kitten's.

The shock of finding herself deposited back on the sofa woke her sharply from her dream. His

hands were brisk, almost businesslike as he ordered
her dishevelled clothing, pulling her dress into place
and re-closing the zip.

Then he got to his feet. He said quietly, and
evenly, 'Now that—*that*—is what all the fuss is
about. Goodnight, Amanda.'

He gave her a brief smile, then walked to the
door, and went out, leaving her to stare after him
in anguished disbelief.

'You're almost a stranger these days.' Mrs Conroy's
voice was plaintive, and Amanda smothered a sigh.

'You're welcome to come to Aylesford Green at
any time,' she said, trying to speak gently. 'You
know you've been invited over and over again.'

Mrs Conroy gave her a sad smile. 'You can be
so insensitive sometimes, Amanda, dear. Something you inherited from your father, no doubt.
Don't you realise how painful it is for me to see
you living in that house with that man?'

Amanda's hands balled tensely into fists in the
folds of her skirt. She hung on to her patience with
an effort. 'Mother, please don't start that again.'

'I'm not starting anything,' her mother said
righteously. 'But I'm entitled to my opinion, and
I find it hideous that any child of mine could have—
sold herself for worldly gain.' She shook her head.
'A marriage begun for all the wrong reasons will
never prosper.'

Amanda suppressed a wry smile. For once, she
thought, her mother had been uncannily close to
the target.

'Did you see in the papers how well dear Nigel did in that Swedish rally?' Mrs Conroy pursued eagerly.

'I could hardly avoid it,' Amanda returned neutrally.

She'd been half afraid that his success might revive the stories about her broken engagement and subsequent marriage, but she need not have worried. The newspapers had other, more promising scandals to occupy their attention, as Malory had prophesied. In fact, if she hadn't panicked over Nigel's insidious attempt to re-enter her life, there would have been no need for this marriage at all.

'You're very pale,' Mrs Conroy surveyed her critically. 'And I think you've lost weight, too.' She sniffed. 'Married life, I suppose. Some men have no consideration.'

'Some men,' Amanda agreed levelly. 'Not all.' Her lashes lowered to shut out the sight of the older woman's disapprovingly primmed face. Her mother's idiosyncratic attitude to sex had never bothered her before, but now she wished suddenly, passionately, that Mrs Conroy was different—the sort of mother it was possible to confide in.

But what could she say?

My married life doesn't exist in the way that you think. Malory has made love to me once, and once only, and since that evening a month ago when he taught me more about pleasure in a few short minutes than many women experience in a lifetime, he hasn't touched me or come anywhere near me.

Her mouth twisted ironically. No, she couldn't say that. Mrs Conroy would undoubtedly tell her how fortunate she was not to be 'bothered' in that way.

She picked up her bag, and rose to her feet.

'Going already?' Her mother's mouth turned down discontentedly at the corners.

'I must, I'm afraid. We're giving a reception at the house for some foreign buyers tonight, and I need to get back to check on the arrangements.'

'I should have thought your husband was wealthy enough to employ someone to do that for him,' Mrs Conroy said sourly.

'Oh, he is,' Amanda agreed with a semblance of cheerfulness. 'But he likes me to be involved.'

And as it was the only purpose she fulfilled in his life, she was determined to make the most of it, she thought, as she drove home.

Her mind went back almost obsessively to that night over four weeks ago. When Malory had left her, she'd eventually pulled herself together and gone up to her room. She'd undressed, put on a lacy *peignoir*, and curled up on the window seat. At any moment, she knew, the door would open, and he would come to her—to finish what he'd started in that firelit room downstairs. To make her his completely.

She had woken, chilled and cramped, shortly before dawn, to the shattering realisation that she was still alone. She had crept into bed and lain there, shivering. She had been so sure she would spend the night in his arms. So sure, and so wrong.

When morning came, she had stayed in her room until she was certain he'd left the house, telling herself she couldn't face him—ever. But that had been foolish. She'd been obliged to confront him that evening over the dinner table—and he'd behaved as if nothing had happened. No awkward initial encounter, no recriminations, no passionate aftermath. As if the previous twenty-four hours had been wiped away and they were still—comparative strangers.

As the days passed, Amanda had realised with a kind of shock that this was how Malory intended their relationship to stay. At first, she hadn't been able to comprehend the reason, then eventually the truth dawned on her. Her initiation into the mechanics of sex had not been at all as she'd anticipated, and she'd been too obsessed with her own disappointment to consider Malory's reactions. Now, it occurred to her for the first time that he might have been equally disillusioned, have found her lacking as a lover in all kinds of ways.

And there was no way in which she could argue with that, Amanda acknowledged with a small, bitter sigh, as she turned her car into the drive, and parked at the side of the house. Her sole option now was to fill the role he'd indicated for her in this marriage as efficiently as possible, and stop hoping for anything more. Because, shamingly, she'd come to realise that Malory had aroused needs and longings in her that only he could satisfy.

She'd come an awful long way since those early days when she'd written him off as some kind of neuter, she realised ruefully, as she let herself into the house by the side door. And living here with him, sharing a roof but nothing else, was becoming increasingly painful with every day that passed.

It wasn't as if he was unkind, or dismissive with her. He was just polite and eternally, impenetrably aloof, making it clearer than any direct statement that she no longer held the least physical interest for him.

And that was something she would have to learn, somehow, to endure.

Mrs Priddy met her in the kitchen passage, full of the direst forebodings about the caterers hired for that evening. Amanda reassured her about their reliability and walked on into the utility room, where the flowers for the evening were awaiting her attention. She didn't consider she was particularly artistic, but arranging flowers was one of her great pleasures, and spring flowers in particular were her favourites.

She spent a happy couple of hours experimenting with various containers, then began to carry the results of her labours through to the dining-room and drawing-room.

She was putting some finishing touches to one arrangement, and was too absorbed to be aware she was no longer alone until Nigel's voice said behind her, 'How very charming. You have all kinds of hidden talents, sweetie.'

Amanda cried out, whirling round, her hand pressed to her hammering heart. He was standing there, smiling, looking her over with that slow, sexy surveillance which had always had the power to set her pulses racing.

She steadied her voice. 'How—how did you get in here?'

'Not very welcoming, sister-in-law, dear,' he chided. 'I'm not barred from the house, am I? Old Mal hasn't issued an injunction forbidding me to cross his sacred threshold?'

She disregarded that. 'You startled me. I didn't hear the doorbell.'

'I didn't ring it.' Nigel gestured towards the french windows. 'I came across the gardens, and let myself in that way. I am family, after all.' He paused. 'Aren't you just the tiniest bit pleased to see me?'

She'd wondered often and often what her reaction would be when she saw Nigel again, and now she knew. She felt numb.

She said, 'Why have you come here?'

'To offer my congratulations to the newly-weds.' He smiled at her. 'I suppose I could hardly have expected an invitation to the wedding, under the circumstances. But I'm quite prepared to let bygones be bygones and contribute a wedding present. Although I'm not sure what you give the man who has everything,' he added, giving his surroundings an appraising stare before switching back to Amanda. 'Including, of course, my woman.'

She bit her lip. 'I think it would be better if you left.'

Nigel tutted. 'All this hospitality,' he remarked, looking at the floral displays. 'And none for me. What's the matter, darling? Suffering from a touch of the might-have-beens?'

'No,' she said. 'Just rather busy, that's all.'

He laughed. 'Found your *métier*, have you— sitting at Malory's table—spending his money?

Makes up, does it, for having to let him maul you about once in a while?'

'I said—get out.' Amanda could feel her fingers curling into claws. 'If you want to visit here, please do so when Malory's at home.'

'Thus speaks the virtuous little wife,' he mocked. 'Dullness must be catching, sweetie. You wouldn't have said that before Mal put his boring seal on you.'

Hot angry colour invaded Amanda's face. 'I think you've insulted him enough,' she said. 'Now, will you go, or do I have to call George?'

He flung up his hands in mock surrender. 'OK. I'll leave quietly.' He moved back towards the french windows. 'Want to see me safely off the premises—check my pockets for the family silver?'

Unwillingly, she followed. From now on, she thought, she would keep the french windows locked.

Nigel stepped out into the garden, then turned to look at her.

'You've changed,' he said softly, 'but it's all on the surface, isn't it, Manda? Under the rich wife gloss, you're still the girl I love.' His hand closed with startling suddenness on her wrist, drawing her towards him, pulling her against his body. 'Think about this, darling, next time you're lying underneath old Mal, wondering if he'd notice if you went to sleep.' He bent his head, and his mouth fastened on hers, hotly and greedily.

For a moment, she tensed to struggle, to push him away. But to fight would be to accord him some kind of victory, she realised, would make his assault on her mouth seem more important than it was. And she didn't want to give him even that much satisfaction.

At last, he lifted his head. 'Like kissing a statue,' he said insolently. 'But I suppose that's what marriage to my dear brother does to a woman. See you around, sweetheart.' He patted her cheek, and started away across the lawn.

Amanda stayed where she was, watching him go.

So, it had happened at last, she thought. The moment she'd dreaded. The moment she'd longed for. She'd seen Nigel again, known his touch, and his kiss. And, in spite of her brave words to herself, she'd waited for her starved body to go up in flames.

Only—she hadn't. All she'd been aware of was a certain clinical curiosity about her own lack of response, and a very definite distaste for the feel of his lips sucking at hers—his attempts to push his tongue into her mouth.

All the time I've been afraid, she thought wonderingly, but of what? There's nothing left in me for Nigel—nothing at all. And yet he was my whole life.

She closed the windows and locked them, her hands shaking. There had to be a reason why she'd fallen so completely out of love with Nigel. And suddenly, shatteringly, she knew what it was.

She looked almost bewilderedly round the quiet room. She'd fled here for sanctuary, to this beautiful, tranquil house, or so she'd thought. But the house, however lovely, had only been a shell.

I didn't know it, she thought, but I was running here to Malory all the time. Even then, I must have loved him, long before I knew I wanted him. Before I even knew what wanting could be.

She looked at the bowl of flowers, and it blurred into a mass of indistinct colour.

Well, she knew now, and the knowledge was like an open wound in her soul, because she was neither loved nor desired in return. And she had to live with that for the rest of her life.

CHAPTER NINE

THE reception was at its height. Amanda moved between the laughing, chattering groups of people, her outward smiling serenity belying the torrent of emotion within her. Her life might be in tatters, but the evening was a success, and she had to be satisfied with that, as Malory undoubtedly was.

She was conscious of his presence all the time—aware of every move he made. His understated elegance in dinner-jacket and black tie took her by the throat. She wondered almost hysterically how she could ever have thought him ordinary. Or had she, even then, been fighting an attraction she did not wholly comprehend?

'Hello, Mrs Templeton.' A familiar face materialised at her side, smiling at her. 'I'm Peter Wilton. We met at the company dinner.'

'I remember,' she said instantly. 'You told me about Chromazyn. How's it going?'

He looked momentarily astonished. 'Hasn't Dr Templeton told you? The monitored tests are proceeding extraordinarily well. No unexpected side-effects, or any other disasters, touch wood.'

Amanda laughed. 'Now there's an unscientific reaction,' she teased.

'Oh, I'm all for a little superstition,' he said, grinning back at her. 'All medicine has an element of magic, after all. And sometimes we need all the help we can get. And a fair amount of luck, too.' He paused. 'So many drugs have been hailed as breakthroughs—miracles one day and condemned the next, often with damaging lawsuits attached. Hopefully, that won't happen to Chromazyn.'

They exchanged a few more words, then Amanda turned away, to find her path blocked by Malory, who had been standing a few feet away from her.

He'd been late back from the laboratories that evening, and had only arrived downstairs in his evening clothes in time to greet their first guests, so they'd hardly had a chance to say two words to each other. And he hadn't been able to pay her the pleasantly distant compliment on her appearance that he usually did on these occasions.

Now, suddenly, they were face to face. His eyes were narrowed as he surveyed her in the square-necked midnight-blue dress which she knew, without conceit, gave her the look of a medieval princess, moulding itself to her slender figure down to the hips, where the floor-length skirt flared slightly, the effect heightened by a draped sash belt, embroidered in gold. Her uncertain, rather shy smile died on her lips, as her stunned mind registered the swift, dark stain of colour along his cheekbones, the stark, burning hunger which blazed momentarily in his face, then was hidden behind the normal polite mask.

As he turned on his heel, and walked away, she found she was gasping. He wasn't indifferent to her, she thought shakily. He wasn't. That brief, unguarded moment had been too revealing. He still wanted her. After all—in spite of everything—he did want her. She grabbed a glass from a passing tray, and took a swift gulp of champagne.

Then why, *why*, she wailed inwardly, had he kept her at more than arm's length all these endless weeks? And what guarantee was there that he wouldn't continue to do so? Just because he'd let the mask slip a little didn't mean that he would allow his body to dictate to his mind. He was, she knew, far too fastidious for that.

And, besides, he had no means of knowing about her own moment of self-revelation. No means at all, unless she let him know—somehow.

'Lovely party,' an American voice said, and her smile flashed as if it was on auto-pilot.

In a way, she wished the reception was a dismal failure. That way, they would all leave, and she could be alone with him.

No, she thought. She would just be alone. When the house was empty, Malory would excuse himself courteously, as he always did, and leave her to her solitude. And if she threw herself at him, as she'd done that last disastrous time, he might well throw her back.

I can't risk that, she thought, exchanging hesitant banalities with a Japanese couple. But what other choice do I have?

She didn't care if she was being a lousy hostess. She had to find him. Eventually, she tracked him down in his study, seated in a group around the fire.

Taking her courage in both hands, she sat down on the arm of his chair, sliding her arm intimately across its back, leaning sideways towards him so that he was aware of her warmth, her scent. To a casual observer, she was being an ordinary, affectionate wife. Only Malory knew differently, and she could feel his awareness in his sudden tension, although he continued to talk with outward calmness to his guests.

But he knew, and she knew that he knew, he would only have to turn his head slightly for his cheek to graze the curve of her breast—move his hand a fraction for it to rest on her thigh.

She stayed long enough to etch her acceptance, her readiness, on his consciousness, then drifted away again.

And this time, he followed her. As she talked and laughed, and made sure plates and glasses remained filled, Malory was there on the edge of her vision, watching as if he could not bear to take his eyes off her. And she used his regard quite shamelessly, every turn, every movement of her body totally deliberate, designed to inflame him beyond all bearing.

What she could not gauge was the extent to which she was succeeding. She dared not look at him directly, because she knew if she did that her gaze might plead, and that wasn't what she intended at all. Tonight they would meet, if at all, on equal terms.

She was no longer the complete innocent. She had been allowed a glimpse of the extent of her own sensuality. Now, her body was awakened, urgent, seeking to test those limits to the full.

The only glances she sent his way, were brief, and loaded, under demurely lowered lashes.

The evening seemed endless. It was long past midnight when people began reluctantly to take their leave. She shook hands, and smiled, and pantomimed a regret she did not feel. The Templeton executives at the reception lingered endlessly, their mood clearly euphoric. It was difficult concealing her impatience to see the back of them.

I shall just, she thought, have to concentrate on something else. And, in turn, she began to watch her husband overtly, allowing her eyes to slide down his body, as if mentally reminding herself of what he looked like without his clothes. She was perfectly discreet, of course. Only Malory knew what she was up to, and the taut lines of his face revealed the effect it was having on him.

Peter Wilton was among the last to leave. Amanda had already given instructions that any clearing up was to be delayed until the following morning. Now, knowing that Malory was outside, saying goodnight, guiding the last cars out of the drive, she went swiftly and noiselessly upstairs. She went straight to Malory's room, switching on one of the big lamps which flanked the bed. Then she kicked off her shoes, unfastening and taking down her stockings, before beginning without haste to undo her dress.

She didn't hear Malory's approach up the stairs, and she didn't look towards the doorway, yet instinct told her that he was there, watching her as if in a trance.

She let the midnight dress fall in a shimmering pool round her feet, and stood motionless for a moment in the silken teddy which was all she wore beneath it, before putting up her hands to unpin her piled-up hair, letting it fall round her shoulders.

Then, and only then, she looked at him, her body poised in a challenge as old as mankind.

He might have been carved out of stone. Only the blue eyes flared with an icy flame. When at last he made a movement, it was a brief, imperative gesture that told her without words that even the fragile veiling of the teddy was too much of a barrier to his eyes.

She obeyed instantly, dealing with the simple fastenings, slipping the ribbon straps down from her shoulders so that the flimsy garment joined the remainder of her clothing on the floor.

He came to her then, and, as he lifted her into his arms, she pressed her lips to his throat with a little sigh of surrender.

He put her down on the bed, and knelt above her, wrenching his clothing apart. He kissed her once, his lips parting hers with demanding mastery, then their bodies joined in a tense, trembling silence.

Amanda had prepared herself for more pain, but there was none—only a sense of total, almost over-whelming completion. She drew him down, drew him into her ever more deeply, every sense attuned to this miracle they were making together.

Almost before she had believed it possible, she was seized, rent apart by a pleasure so intense it bordered on agony. She heard herself crying out her incoherent delight against his mouth as the spasms tore through her, then ebbed, leaving her adrift on some tideless sea of languid contentment.

For a few moments Malory lay cradling her in his arms, then he moved, withdrawing from her, and her eyes opened in panic. He laid a finger on her lips, silencing her protest, before beginning to undress, his movements urgent and rapid, his eyes never leaving her face.

When he came back into her arms, he started to kiss her very gently, his lips bestowing a tracery of magic on her face, throat and breasts.

The breath sighed between her lips, as, incredibly, she felt the hot, slow excitement begin to build in her again.

That first time, she realised, had been born of mutual desperation. This time, it would be very different. This time, she was being seduced.

Malory's mouth travelled without haste down her body, exploring every curve and crevice, his tongue flickering fire across her tumescent nipples, circling her navel with teasing eroticism. He kissed the length of her thighs, the soft inner bend of her knee, her insteps, her pink-polished toes. Every nerve-ending she possessed seemed to be vibrating to the leisurely brush of his lips.

For the first time, she understood the words from the Marriage Service—*with my body, I thee worship*.

Malory was worshipping her, she realised dazedly, with a warm and tender sensuality which left her breathless. And the staggering thing was that he hadn't yet sought any satisfaction for himself.

She tried to speak, but again he silenced her, this time with his mouth. His hands were moving on her now, caressing and arousing, and her body twisted restlessly, mutely demanding appeasement.

Malory turned suddenly on to his back, lifting her over him, drawing her down so that her body sheathed him, silk against his velvet hardness. She looked down at him, her eyes widening as she assimilated this new and devastating sensation, then an instinct she hadn't known she possessed took over, and she began to move on him in sweet and sensuous rhythm, letting her hair swing round her love-flushed face like a scented chestnut curtain.

When, at last, he groaned in ecstasy, his head twisting on the pillow, the muscles in his throat standing out like cords, Amanda felt as if she'd been awarded the most glittering prize of all.

This time Malory didn't try to separate from her. They lay, wrapped in each other's arms, exchanging slow, delicious kisses, Amanda's hands becoming more adventurous as she began to stroke and explore his body in turn.

No such thing as instant bliss, she thought languorously. How could he have denied it when he made her feel like this—when he himself could want her again, so unmistakably, and so soon?

And, as their mutual need began to build again, she stopped thinking at all.

Hours later, she woke in his arms with the grey light of morning gleaming outside the window. She lay for a while, savouring the strong, unhurried beat of his heart under her cheek. She had not, she thought drowsily, told him yet that she loved him, and that was a serious omission. But then, neither of them had spoken at all for the whole duration of that intense and passionate lovemaking.

She could always wake him now, of course, perhaps by biting him very softly and delicately on the shoulder. And then, perhaps...

She smiled to herself.

Don't be greedy, she adjured herself self-mockingly. He deserves his sleep. And I can tell him how I feel later. After all, this is the real beginning of our marriage—of our life together.

She gave a small, happy sigh, and slept again herself.

The next time she woke, the room was filled with pale and watery sunlight. Amanda reached sleepily for Malory, her eyes flying open in startled reaction as she realised she was alone in the big bed.

She sat up, pushing her hair back, and looking at her watch. It was late, but it was Saturday, and Malory didn't need to go to Templeton's today, so where was he?

She'd slept, her body moulded to the curve of his. She'd wanted to wake in his arms today, of all days, and she was conscious of a stab of disappointment that he'd apparently found it so easy to leave her.

Perhaps the night they'd just spent had not been as important to him as it had to her, a sly inner voice suggested, and she recoiled from the thought.

At the same time, she had to admit that Malory couldn't have learned his undoubted sexual expertise solely from textbooks. Other women, before herself, must have sobbed their delight in his arms.

So perhaps he could afford to be blasé about her joyous and wanton response to his lovemaking.

Oh, stop it, she told herself impatiently as she threw back the covers and swung her feet to the floor. He left me to sleep late, and that's all there is to it.

She gathered up her clothes and retreated to her own room. Half an hour later, bathed and dressed in slim-fitting corded jeans and a cream roll-necked sweater, she ran downstairs, expecting to find Malory there. But he wasn't in his study, or the drawing-room, and any hopes that he might simply be out taking the dog for a walk were extinguished when she entered the kitchen to find Harvey snoring in his basket near the Aga.

Mrs Priddy, who was making pastry, welcomed her placidly with the news that the caterers had removed the last of their equipment, and the house was back to normal.

'So there was no need for you to get up so soon at all, madam,' she told Amanda severely. 'Dr Templeton said you'd had a very late night, and needed to rest.'

Amanda suppressed a giggle inside her. 'Has he gone out?' she asked.

Mrs Priddy nodded. 'Two hours ago, madam.'

'To the laboratories?'

'He didn't say, I'm afraid, Mrs Templeton.' Mrs Priddy gave her a comfortable smile. 'Now, can I get you some breakfast?'

Amanda stifled a sigh. 'I—I don't think so, thanks. Just some coffee would be fine.' Suddenly she didn't feel like giggling any more. She felt almost bereft.

The phone rang several times during the hour that followed. Each time Amanda answered it, her heart lifting in excitement, but each time it was a bread-and-butter call of thanks from someone who'd been at her party.

Eventually, Amanda decided she was sick and tired of roaming round the house like a caged animal, waiting on tenterhooks for her husband's return. She would put some of her brimming energy to good use, and take Harvey for a long walk across the fields. And, if Malory came back while she was out, then he could wait for her for a change.

Harvey was clearly delighted at the scheme, although Mrs Priddy clucked reproachfully over Amanda's announcement that she would dispense with lunch, and have a snack when she returned.

When she returned, cheeks glowing, two hours later, it was to find Malory's car standing in the drive, and her spirits rose magically as she ran into the house.

He was just coming downstairs, and her eager rush to him was halted when she saw he was carrying a suitcase, and had an airline bag slung over his shoulder. She stood still, the warmth and excitement dying out of her face under his cool, unsmiling regard.

Amanda swallowed. 'You—you're going somewhere?' she ventured inanely.

'Unfortunately, yes.' This formal stranger couldn't be the man who'd scaled pleasure's heights with her the previous night, she thought with total incredulity. 'I find I have to go to America.'

'But you didn't say anything about it last . . .' She stopped, and substituted, 'Yesterday.'

'A last-minute change of plan, and quite unavoidable, I'm afraid.' He sounded almost bored, and not in the least apologetic.

'How—how long will you be away?' To her horror, Amanda found it an effort to keep her voice steady.

'It's difficult to say.' Malory clearly had no such problem. 'A matter of weeks rather than days, I imagine.' He glanced at his watch. 'And I'll have to hurry if I want to catch the next flight. You'll have to excuse me.'

She couldn't believe this was happening. One quivering, wretched part of her mind was urging her to fling herself at his feet and beg him to take her with him—on a later flight, if necessary. But her last remnants of pride, and a very real fear of his refusal, kept her silent.

She summoned a smile from somewhere. 'Well, as they say, have a nice day.' Lifting her chin, she turned and walked away into the drawing-room, Harvey following her, tail down, aware that all was not well in his world.

She stood, staring out of the window, looking at the green spikes of bulbs showing above the dark earth—proof, if she needed it, that even if she was dying inside, life went on. Waiting, hoping that Malory would drop those damned cases and come after her. That he'd take her in his arms and tell her with love and yearning why he had to leave her behind at this emotional turning-point in their lives.

One word, she prayed silently. One word of need and regret was all she asked from him.

The sound of the front door closing behind him was like a whiplash across her wincing senses. And presently the sound of the car engine receding into the distance warned her with chilling finality that there was nothing left to hope for.

It was the most wretched day Amanda had ever spent. She wandered from room to room, Harvey pattering after her, feeling more lost, bewildered and alone than she had ever thought possible.

If it hadn't been for the small, intimate marks of lovemaking that Malory had left in significant places on her skin, she would have thought she'd dreamed the whole of the previous night. And the optimism she'd experienced about their future relationship seemed, in retrospect, absurd to the point of tragedy.

She even found herself wondering miserably if she'd transgressed some unknown code, behaved more like a mistress than a wife, embarrassed and shocked him by her wild, uninhibited abandonment to his loving. But she soon dismissed the idea. If she'd been an over-eager pupil, then Malory had been her more-than-willing teacher. And it would be hypocritical in the extreme for him, afterwards, to draw back in distaste from the memory of her response to him. He might be complex, but Amanda didn't believe for one minute he was a hypocrite.

All she could suppose, even more depressingly, was that their night together had not been sufficiently memorable for him to wish to make her his wife in any real sense. He'd had her, and now it was over, and they could revert to the terms of their original agreement.

But I can't, she thought desolately. I can't live as a stranger with him any longer. I want him—I need him too much.

Nor was it merely passion that she longed for from him. It was everything that made a marriage—the laughter, the tenderness, the communication, and the sharing. All the things she had naïvely thought would follow from their loving as spring followed winter.

There was the sourness of unshed tears in her throat. She had thought happiness was hers for the taking, but her hands were empty, and so was her life.

Her reverie was interrupted by the indignant arrival of Mrs Priddy.

'Those florists,' she said scornfully, surging into the room. 'Really, you can't trust anyone these days. Look what George found pushed into one of the dustbins, madam.'

She produced from behind her back, with the air of a conjuror, a magnificent bouquet of long-stemmed red roses, each bloom tightly furled into a dark velvet bud.

'They're lovely.' Amanda touched the protective cellophane covering. 'And they're still absolutely fresh. But I certainly didn't order them. There's clearly been some mistake. Perhaps you'd phone the florist and ask them to collect them.'

'An expensive mistake, if you ask me. And I phoned as soon as George brought them in, Mrs Templeton. But the manageress says she knows nothing about them.' She snorted. 'Fine thing. You want to check their bill when it comes in, in case they do suddenly remember them after all, and charge you.' She gave Amanda a shrewd look. 'Anyway, as they're here, madam, why don't you put them in water? They might cheer you up a little.'

She put the bouquet down on the table, and went back to the kitchen.

It would take, Amanda thought listlessly, more than roses. But the flowers, whoever they'd been intended for, were exquisite, and it would be a shame to let them die.

She removed the wrapping, inhaling the faint scent that wafted to her. Red roses, she thought. A token of love which would never, now, reach its destination. It seemed, somehow the final, sad straw; bending her head, she began, very quietly, to cry.

CHAPTER TEN

THE telephone was ringing as Amanda came into the house. Stripping off her gloves, she called, 'I'll get it,' to Mrs Priddy.

She had no idea what the time difference was between England and America, but she had long ago given up the hope that Malory might be calling her. He had been gone for almost a fortnight, and in that time, hurtfully, there'd been no word from him.

Lifting the receiver, she gave the number.

'Mrs Templeton?' Peter Wilton spoke uncertainly. 'I'm sorry to bother you, but I was wondering if you had any idea where we could contact your husband.'

She said constrictedly. 'But surely his secretary will have an itinerary?'

'Actually, she hasn't—as it's a private visit.' He gave an awkward laugh. 'As a matter of fact, I could have sworn Dr Templeton said you were going with him. He loves the USA, and he was talking about showing you all the places he likes best.' He paused. 'But obviously I've got hold of the wrong end of the stick, yet again, so if you do have an address where we could reach him, I'd be grateful. It is urgent.'

Amanda bit her lip. 'I'm afraid I haven't the least idea where he's staying. He—he left in rather a hurry. . .' She hesitated. 'But I could have a look in the diary in the study, if that would help.'

'That would be marvellous.' His voice was a shade too hearty, and she winced a little as she put the phone down.

The study was in its usual state of immaculate tidiness, and it was the work of seconds to find the diary, and check that it was enigmatically blank on the subject of Malory's whereabouts.

Amanda looked round with a sigh. Surely there would be something to give a clue, she thought. An airline folder, perhaps, or a hotel brochure. She tried the desk drawers, but they were locked, and with a shrug she went back to the phone and admitted defeat.

'Well, it will be all right. We'll trace him ourselves. He's bound to have been in touch with some of our contacts in the States.'

'Yes,' she said, and thought, *but not with his own wife*. She cleared her throat. 'May I know why you want him? You said it was urgent.'

His voice sobered. 'Yes, I'm afraid so. Do you remember my telling you that the Chromazyn tests were going well? It seems I spoke too soon. We've just been notified that one of the patients using the drug has suffered a severe adverse reaction.'

Amanda caught her breath. 'How bad is it?'

'As bad as it's possible to get,' he said grimly. 'She's been having convulsions. They don't think she's going to live. And Dr Templeton has to know about it, naturally.'

'Naturally,' she echoed unhappily. 'I—I just wish I could have been more help.'

'It doesn't matter.' He paused again. 'And Mrs Templeton—try not to worry too much.'

But that was easily said. Amanda went into the drawing-room and sank down on one of the sofas. She was being bombarded with one shock after another, it seemed. But perhaps the news her doctor had just given her would help to alleviate some of Malory's inevitable distress over the Chromazyn crisis, she thought, placing a protective hand on her abdomen.

At first, she'd put her faint feeling of nausea and general malaise down to being lonely and unhappy, but the realisation that her normal monthly cycle had been interrupted, too, had sent her hastily for an appointment with the local GP. And today she had received the positive results of the tests he'd done.

At first, she'd been overjoyed to learn she was pregnant. Then, as she'd driven home, more sobering thoughts had intervened. The coming of a child would make this 'non-marriage', as Malory had called it, far less easy to walk away from. She swallowed. Although Malory had seemed to experience little difficulty in distancing himself from it . . .

And he had told her bluntly that he was not particularly paternal. Might he not regard the baby simply as an inconvenience to hold him trapped in an empty and meaningless relationship?

She must have conceived that very first time she had gone to him, she thought, and wondered what the odds were against that happening. Although, if either of them had been thinking clearly that day, they would have realised some kind of precautions were necessary.

She sighed. Well, it was too late to worry about that now. The baby existed, and she wanted it—especially as it was all of Malory she might ever have. Pain tore through her at the thought, but it was something she had to face. His continuing absence had taught her that quite unequivocally.

But now, if Templeton's made contact with him, he would be coming home, and some basis for their future relationship would have to be formulated.

She allowed forty-eight hours to go by before phoning the laboratories to see if there was any news of Malory. She spoke to his secretary, a pleasant middle-aged woman called Deirdre who did her best to hide her surprise that her boss's wife should be in such complete ignorance about his movements, but did not completely succeed.

Dr Templeton was flying into Heathrow that afternoon, Amanda was told, and she was supplied with the flight number and projected arrival time.

'We'll be sending a car to meet him, Mrs Templeton,' Deirdre went on. 'Unless you plan to do that yourself.'

Amanda said haltingly, 'No, I don't think——Make whatever arrangements seem best.'

Coward, she castigated herself, as she put the phone down. You should make the effort—go and meet him. At least it would remind him that you exist.

She bit her lip. She didn't want to ring the laboratories and tell them meekly she'd changed her mind. There was probably enough discreet speculation going on already. But she could get the train to London, and then a taxi to Heathrow. If she simply turned up, Malory could hardly refuse to give her a lift back, and they could talk.

I can't just stay here, she thought, as if I was waiting for some kind of axe to fall.

She dressed carefully for their meeting, putting on an elegantly cut cream suit, with a long jacket, teaming it with a high-necked turquoise silk blouse. She did her best for her wan face with blusher and eye shadow, but the end result, she was forced to admit, didn't even approach the kind of radiance she wanted to pretend.

Her train was delayed, and the traffic was heavy, so she was late and breathless by the time she arrived at the terminal. Malory's flight arrival had already been announced, and the first passengers were already beginning to filter through.

Amanda stationed herself beside a convenient pillar, miserably aware that her mouth was dry and her palms were damp. And what was she going to say to him when he did appear? 'Oh, hello' was too prosaic, and 'Surprise, surprise' far too flip.

In a perfect world, she thought, his arms would open to her, and she would fling herself into them, and all difficulties and estrangement would vanish like morning mist, without need for words. She could only pray that, when the time came, she would find the right thing to say.

Then she saw him and, in spite of her nervousness, her heart began to thud with heavy, sweet excitement.

He was smiling, and for one absurd, joyous moment Amanda thought he'd seen her through the crowd, and was pleased. Then he glanced down and she saw his lips moving, and for the first time she realised he was not alone.

The breath seemed to stop in her throat. People had moved, giving her a clear view of his approach. And of the girl walking by his side.

Last time Amanda had seen her, she had been naked, but today she was elegant in black, a fun-fur coat thrown around her shoulders, the beautiful face, framed in heavy blonde hair, bright and animated as she looked up at him.

Sudden, terrifying nausea scaled Amanda's throat. All she could think was, They mustn't see me—they mustn't...

The agony of seeing Malory with Clare was enough. She couldn't bear any further humiliation. She turned clumsily, blundering into someone.

''Ere, look where you're going, darling,' an aggrieved voice reprimanded her, and she murmured an attempt at an apology as she continued her headlong flight.

Somehow, she found herself in the fresh air, gulping great lungfuls of it as she fought off the faintness which threatened to overwhelm her.

'Someone I'd come to think of as mine.' Malory's words seemed to beat at her brain. And now Clare was his again. Leaving her hurt and frightened, and out in the cold.

'If you want him,' Jane said gently, 'then fight for him.'

Amanda looked at her blankly. 'Fight?' she echoed bitterly. 'With what?'

'Oh, come on.' Jane's tone was bracing. 'Let's not have any false modesty. You're a beautiful girl. You're also his wife, and possession is supposed to be nine points of the law. And you're expecting his baby. Game, set and match.'

'But he prefers her.' She could hardly bear to say it. The realisation that Malory had gone from that sweet, fierce, passionate night with her straight to Clare's arms seared at her. She had not believed him capable of such cynicism. But then, how well did she really know him? she thought with desperate weariness.

'You don't know that,' Jane said. 'There might be some completely innocent explanation for them being together.'

Amanda said bleakly. 'Can you think of one?'

'No,' Jane admitted, and there was a depressed silence. Finally, Jane said, 'Are you sure you want to go back tonight? Wouldn't you rather stay here—pull yourself together a little before you have to face him?'

Amanda shook her head. 'I'd only have to embark on long explanations for Maggie and Fiona, and I don't think I'm up to that. I'd better go.' She gave Jane a faint smile. 'Thanks for being an angel, and letting me weep on your shoulder, metaphorically speaking.'

'The shoulder is always there.' Jane's face was sober. 'You know, I don't think I've ever felt so disappointed in anyone. I only met Malory a couple of times, I know, but I would have sworn he wasn't that kind of man.'

So would I, Amanda thought heavily. So would I.

The journey back to Aylesford Green seemed endless. It was a slow train and stopped everywhere. And when the local taxi dropped her at the house, she discovered from Mrs Priddy that Malory had telephoned to say he would not be returning that night.

From some inner reserve she hadn't known she possessed, she managed to thank her quietly and walk upstairs to her room without collapsing.

She had wept over Nigel, but Malory's betrayal seemed too deep, too wounding for tears.

She undressed and got into bed, lying for hours, staring into the darkness. She had to try and make some plans, decide whether she could endure living under Malory's roof, knowing that he would not be faithful to her, or if it would be better to leave, with whatever dregs of pride she could salvage.

But where would she go? she asked herself, her body tossing restlessly. Her spirit quailed at the prospect of returning to the cottage and her mother's recriminations. And she had reached no concrete decision by the time she dropped into an uneasy doze shortly before dawn.

She was woken the next morning by Mrs Priddy, bearing a breakfast tray.

'Because you haven't been eating properly lately,' that redoubtable lady declared, putting the tray firmly on Amanda's lap. 'Now you polish off every scrap.'

Amanda looked at the freshly squeezed orange juice, and the shiny brown egg in its silver cup, with attendant toast soldiers, and she didn't know whether to laugh or cry.

'And Dr Templeton's back.' Mrs Priddy added, forestalling the question Amanda had been afraid to ask. 'He arrived half an hour since.' She gave Amanda an encouraging nod and left.

Amanda ate what she was capable of, then pushed the tray away. The sooner she saw Malory—confronted him—the better, she thought without conviction.

His study door was firmly closed, and for a moment she was tempted to knock. Then she rallied herself. She was his wife, not some employee, after all.

He was sitting at his desk, glancing through his papers, and he looked deathly tired, she thought with swift compassion, until she suddenly remembered the probable cause of those deep shadows under his eyes.

'Good morning.' His greeting was polite and totally without warmth. 'Is there something I can do for you, Amanda?'

This was going to be even worse than she'd feared. She drew a breath, and wished she wasn't shaking so much inside. 'I—I need to talk to you. There's something you should know.'

'Ah,' he said softly. 'Could it be, I wonder, that you're having a baby?'

Amanda's jaw dropped. 'How—how did you know?'

The blue eyes were glacial as he looked at her. 'Because it's the only explanation that makes a kind of obscene sense.' He paused, twisting a pen between his fingers. 'So tell me the rest, Amanda. Who's the proud father?'

The question was so totally unexpected that, for a moment, her mind refused to work. She said, stumblingly, 'I—I don't understand what you mean.'

'It's not really that difficult. You are expecting a child, whose upbringing and education will be my ultimate responsibility. Out of interest, I'd like to know if I gave it life, or whether it was Nigel.'

Her lips felt numb. 'But it's yours—you know it is. You know I was a virgin when we—when you...'

'I'm not likely to forget that less than glorious moment,' he said curtly. 'But you've had plenty of time since then to test your sexual emancipation. And let's not pretend Nigel hasn't visited you here.'

Amanda had been reeling, but now a small coil of anger began to spiral inside her.

'And what if he has?' Her voice shook. 'You're hardly in a position to throw the first stone.'

'Meaning what, precisely?'

'Meaning that I was at Heathrow yesterday. I—I recognised your companion.' She flung her head back. 'Did you enjoy showing her your favourite America?' The thought made her temper flare into the danger zone. 'So—how did you find Nigel's leavings?'

For a long moment he looked at her, and she saw a little muscle flicker beside his mouth. Then he said, too evenly, 'Judge for yourself.'

He opened the drawer beside him and extracted a manila envelope which he pushed across the desk at her. It was, she realised, the kind of cardboard backed envelope which normally contained photographs, and this was no exception.

The top one was more than explicit. It showed Nigel and herself framed in the french windows, kissing. The next two were variations on the same theme. The last showed Amanda on her own, her expression tender, wistful, luminous. The face of a girl dreaming of her lover.

In a way, that was the most damaging of all.

She said slowly, 'Where did these come from?'

'The postman brought them—the very morning after you'd taken me to paradise and back.' There was a jeering bitterness in his voice. 'I should have remembered that every Eden has its serpent— should have asked myself why you were so gratifyingly eager to go to bed with me.' He smiled without amusement. 'But your friend with the candid camera made it crystal clear why you could be in need of some—physical alibi. You'd realised, of course, that your romantic interlude could have consequences.' He added courteously, 'I hope he lived up to all your expectations as a lover.'

She remembered, with a feeling of sickness, Nigel's mouth mauling hers, his hands groping at her, and stifled a shudder.

She said quietly, 'Yes, he did—in every way.' She put the photographs back in the envelope and laid them down on the desk. 'There—there isn't a great deal more to be said, is there?'

She didn't wait for his answer, but went swiftly out of the room, closing the door behind her. She let herself out of the house, and began to walk aimlessly down the drive, trying to make sense of what had just happened.

She had been set up by Nigel—that went without saying. The kiss had been staged deliberately for the benefit of the photographer—one of his Fleet Street cronies, no doubt—who'd been hidden among the evergreens on the far side of the lawn. The film wouldn't have taken long to develop, and the resulting prints would have caught the last post without difficulty—to reach Malory, by some hideous coincidence, on that one morning of all mornings, and poison the memory of their night together.

She forced down the little moan which rose in her throat. And it provided a cogent explanation for his renewed relationship with Clare. If she had a lover, after all, there was no reason why he shouldn't take a mistress. She could understand the cynical logic which had inspired his decision. Could even forgive it—except that her forgiveness was not required.

She shivered, wrapping her arms round her body.

But what did he want? He'd spoken of the baby being his responsibility, but he couldn't expect her to go on living with him in some terrible atmosphere of bitterness and distrust.

Her throat closed convulsively. When she could face him again, she would tell him she wanted a legal separation. And she would make it clear at the same time that she wanted no financial support from him, then or in the future. There were thousands of single parents managing to get along somehow, and she would be one of them, she thought fiercely.

There was a warning bark, and Harvey joined her, panting cheerfully. With a sinking heart, Amanda realised she hadn't closed the front door properly.

'You bad lad.' She tried to catch at his collar. 'Go back. You know you're not allowed out without your lead.'

But whatever Harvey knew, he had scented freedom, and was not to be baulked of it. He set off towards the gates, which were also ajar, with Amanda in frantic pursuit, his barks becoming hysterical when he realised there was a cat crouching on the opposite verge.

As he gained the road, Amanda made a grab for him, her feet sliding on the damp surface. 'Harv, you horror...'

She heard the sound of the van coming too fast round the corner, the blare of its horn, and caught a glimpse of the driver's horrified face as he swerved to avoid them.

With all her strength, she pushed Harvey back towards the gate, and his startled yelp was the last thing she heard as the van's front wing struck her a glancing blow, and the world turned in a slow, sickening arc, and became darkness.

CHAPTER ELEVEN

'How do you feel, Mrs Templeton?' The quiet voice pierced the aching fog which seemed to surround her.

She mumbled, 'I hurt.'

'I'm not surprised.' She opened her eyes to see a bearded man in a white coat looking down at her. 'You took a very nasty tumble. You've got a considerable number of cuts, bruises and abrasions, and a possible mild concussion. That's why we thought it might be better to look after you here for a day or two—with your condition to take into account.'

Her lips trembled. 'I've—lost the baby, haven't I?'

'Good lord, no,' he said cheerfully. 'Miscarriages aren't inevitable after accidents, you know. You're a strong, healthy girl, and that baby's firmly ensconced.'

Amanda closed her eyes again. Unbidden, the thought came to her, *It might have been better if...* and she stopped there, rejecting it savagely.

She said, 'Where am I?'

He mentioned the private wing of a famous London teaching hospital. 'You were transferred from the casualty department of your own cottage hospital,' he added.

'Have I been unconscious?'

He laughed. 'Well, not all the time. But if you'll promise to stay awake for a few minutes longer, I'll fetch your husband. He's been very patient, but I think your Sleeping Beauty act has started to get to him.'

Amanda parted her lips to protest, but the doctor was already moving briskly to the door. When he returned, Malory was with him.

He was very pale, the lines of strain marked on his face. He bent and kissed her on the forehead.

'How are you?' He looked gravely down at her.

'I'm all right.' She saw the doctor remove himself tactfully from the room.

Malory pulled forward a chair, and sat down. 'You've had a raw deal from the Templetons.' He gave her a small, bitter smile. 'Nigel nearly sent you off a bridge. I succeeded in throwing you under a van.'

'It wasn't like that.' She moved her head in negation, and winced. 'Is—is Harvey all right?'

'Apart from being in total disgrace, he's flourishing.'

'Poor Harvey.'

'Damn Harvey!' he said with sudden violence. 'You could have been killed.'

I wish I had been. She didn't say it, but he must have read it in her face, because he reached and took her hand in his.

'You're going to be fine,' he said gently. 'And so is the baby. Nothing matters but that.'

A lot of things mattered, she thought unhappily.

She said, 'When they let me leave here, I'd like to go away by myself. You don't have to see me again.'

It was his turn to wince. 'We'll talk about it when you're better.' He released her hand. 'Your mother's up in town, staying with a friend. May I tell her she can visit you this evening?'

'Yes, that would be nice.' And it would remove the onus of visiting from him, she thought. He wouldn't have to sit here, pretending he cared.

But she'd forgotten his former ability to read her mind. He said, 'Actually I'm almost camping here at the moment. Mrs Markham is in intensive care on this floor.'

She frowned, then remembered. 'Oh, the Chromazyn patient. How—how is she?'

'Not too good,' he said curtly. 'And her husband, who couldn't praise us highly enough when the treatment began, is now threatening us with legal action, and the power of the press.' His mouth curled. 'Something on the lines of "They used my dying wife as a guinea pig," or an equally tasteless angle.'

'Why do you think it all went wrong?'

He shrugged tiredly. 'God knows. We've been monitoring her treatment most stringently. We knew there could be a reaction if she took Chromazyn in conjunction with certain other drugs, so that's why we had her in here, so that she couldn't get her hands on even an aspirin tablet that wasn't prescribed.' He sighed. 'Yet, even so, we obviously missed something.'

She said constrictedly, 'I'm sorry. I know you all had high hopes of Chromazyn. I suppose all the tests will have to stop now.'

'Of course. We can't risk the same thing happening again to some other poor soul.' He got to his feet. 'I'd better go. I've been warned not to tire you.' He gave her another brief, formal smile. 'I'll see you tomorrow.'

She wanted to say, 'You don't have to,' but she couldn't force her lips to frame the words. Watching him walk away from her was like bleeding to death.

Her mother's visit was something of an ordeal. Learning that she was to be a grandmother had diametrically changed Mrs Conroy's attitude to Malory. She was full of plans for the baby, names for the baby, and maternal advice for Amanda. She'd even brought some samples of suitable nursery wallpapers with her, and was clearly itching to go to Aylesford Green and choose a room worthy of its future occupant.

If Amanda hadn't been so unhappy, she would have laughed herself into stitches when Mrs Conroy had made her triumphant departure. As it was, she wept a little, and found herself on the receiving end of a reproving lecture from Sister as a result.

'And your husband asked me to tell you that Mrs Markham seems to be taking a turn for the better,' was her valedictory remark.

A stream of flowers and cards began to arrive, and Amanda felt a total fraud. She was stiff and sore, but perfectly well, and Dr Redmond had promised she could leave hospital the day after tomorrow. There were visitors, too. Jane came, and

Peter Wilton, and Mrs Priddy, towing a subdued
George in her wake. She was touched by their
concern, but found herself wondering what they
would think when they realised she and Malory had
parted.

He was punctilious about seeing her, but his visits
were difficult occasions, their conversational exchanges halting and stilted.

She didn't want to remember their marriage like
this, Amanda thought wretchedly each time he left.
She wanted to hold in her heart Malory's gentleness
to her, the sense of belonging he'd taught her, as
well as the other more intimate memories which
tormented her more with every hour that passed.

She was sitting by the window, looking desul-
torily through a fashionable and very expensive
babywear catalogue her mother had given her, when
the door opened and, glancing up, she saw Clare
standing there.

Shock kept her silent for a moment, then she said
huskily, 'I don't know what you're doing here, but
will you please leave?'

'When I've said what I've got to say.' Clare had
an attractive voice, warm and low-pitched.

'Nothing that I want to hear.'

'I wouldn't be too sure,' Clare retorted, then
stopped. She said ruefully. 'Oh, hell, this isn't what
I intended at all. Although I can't altogether blame
you for wanting to throw me out.' She bit her lip.
'I've been having pretty venomous thoughts about
you, too.'

'How fascinating,' Amanda said icily. 'You seduce my fiancé, and have an affair with my husband, and it's all my fault.'

Clare sighed. 'How little you know.' She sat down, crossing shapely legs. 'First things first, Mrs Templeton. I am not having and never have had an affair with Malory. Not that I didn't want to, you understand. That was the problem. I—I was desperate for Malory to take me to bed, but he just doesn't sleep around. And I got the strongest impression that he was only taking me out as camouflage, anyway, because the girl he really wanted was unavailable. Rather damaging to the ego, that.'

She hesitated. 'So when that other bastard came sniffing around, I suppose I was fair game.' She gave Amanda a level look. 'You think I seduced Nigel—dragged him into bed?' She shook her head. 'It was the other way round. He besieged me. Flowers, little gifts, telephone calls, lifts, lunches. You name it, he provided it. And I was flattered. Who wouldn't have been?' She gave a half-smile. 'The expression on your face tells me the treatment sounds familiar.'

'Yes.' It was humiliating to acknowledge it, but Nigel had courted her in much the same way.

'He should have his line patented,' Clare said contemptuously. 'Because that's all it is—a line. A means to an end. A way of getting at Malory, of whom he's always been pathologically jealous.'

She threw back her head, and the blonde hair swung. 'He told me all about it—after you ran away that day, and he was getting dressed to follow you.

He'd always known how to get women into bed, he said, and he'd seduced the first girlfriend Malory had ever brought home to meet his family. It became just like a game, he said. To see a woman that Malory wanted, and move in on her—squeeze him out. Humiliate him. Malory might have been their father's favourite, he told me, but he'd take care that he was always second-best where women were concerned. I was just one in a long line of his successes. He actually laughed about it. And he said, "I can't wait for him to get married. Then I'll really go into action."'

Amanda said, 'Don't—oh, God, don't! No one could be like that.'

Clare said flatly, 'I didn't believe it either, until I saw Malory a couple of days later, and realised he knew exactly what had been going on—and that I hadn't a prayer any more where he was concerned.' She shuddered. 'That was what hurt, not Nigel—I only had myself to blame for that. But the fact that I'd lost Malory through my own blind, egotistical stupidity. If I'd turned Nigel down—if you'd married him—then Malory might have loved me eventually. And I'd have made him happy. Which is more than you're doing.'

Amanda flinched. 'How dare you!'

'Oh, I dare.' Clare's eyes were steely. 'I met him on the plane coming back from New York—I'd been there on a modelling assignment. He looked terrible. I—I asked a few idle questions about Nigel, and watched his reaction.' She took a breath. 'My God, I hated you. I saw you at the airport, although Malory didn't. I saw you running away again, and I was glad. I thought, It serves her right, the silly little bitch. She's got the only man I'll ever want, and she still hankers after his worthless brother.'

'Then why are you here, telling me all this?'

Clare looked down at her nails. 'Because I've seen Nigel—spoken to him. I was in this wine bar, and he was there. He'd been drinking, and I asked him, straight out, what he'd been up to. He looked smug, and said he'd fixed things so that Malory would never trust you again. He went rambling on about some production of *Othello* he'd seen years before, and the value of circumstantial evidence.' She sent Amanda a narrow-eyed look. 'I didn't know what the hell he was talking about, but clearly you do.'

Amanda flushed. 'Yes.'

'Then, presumably, you also know how to deal with it. Unless, of course, you really are still carrying a torch for that little swine.'

Amanda shuddered. 'God, no!' She looked down at her clasped hands. 'But it's too late to save my marriage.'

'So what are you going to do about it—run away for the third time?' Clare's tone jeered at her. Her smile was catlike. 'That would suit me very well. With you out of the way, Malory might turn to me again.'

Amanda's head lifted sharply, and she stared at the older girl. She said, grittily, 'I really wouldn't count on it.'

Clare gave a meditative nod. 'So, you do love him,' she said. 'I admit, I'd wondered.' Her smile wavered. 'And he loves you, even if he is bleeding to death at the moment. He gave me a lift from the airport—my idea, not his—and in the car, I—I made it clear I was his for the asking, that I'd console him in any way he wanted.' She sighed. 'He was still polite, still charming, and, physically, he didn't move a muscle. Yet suddenly he was a thousand miles away.' There was a pause, then briskly she pulled herself together. 'Well, Mrs Templeton, goodbye, and good luck.'

Amanda watched the door close behind Clare and thought, I'm going to need it.

When Dr Redmond made his rounds, Amanda told him quietly and firmly that she wished to discharge herself and return home. She was aware that Malory had followed him into the room, and she avoided his gaze as Dr Redmond debated her request.

'Well, why not?' he said at last. 'But you must promise me to take things easy for the next few days, spend as much time in bed as possible.'

Malory said, with a ghost of a laugh in his voice, 'No problem,' and Amanda looked down at her hands, folded in her lap, forbidding herself to blush.

But did he mean it, she asked herself confusedly as a hired car drove her to Aylesford Green, or was he simply presenting the façade of a happy marriage to the world? Certainly, the remark was the most human he'd made in days.

Mrs Priddy was hovering anxiously on the step, her face splitting with a smile as Amanda was helped out of the car.

'The master rang with his orders,' she told Amanda firmly. 'It's a nice, warm bath for you, then your dinner on a tray in bed, and no argument.'

When Amanda reached the top of the stairs, she turned automatically towards the west room, but Mrs Priddy halted her, her face pinkening slightly.

'Mr Malory also gave instructions for your things to be moved to his own room, madam,' she said. 'I hope that was right.'

'Oh, yes,' Amanda returned rather faintly. 'Quite—right.'

Bathed, clad in her best nightgown, she sat propped up by pillows and ate her dinner obediently, and waited on tenterhooks for Malory's return.

It was late when she eventually heard the sound of the car. And it seemed an eternity before the bedroom door opened, and he came in.

He stood for a long moment, staring at her, Then he said quietly, 'Welcome home.'

'Thank you.' She gave him an uncertain smile. He still looked pale, but there was a new air of relaxation about him. She said with sudden insight, 'Mrs Markham—something's happened.'

He nodded. 'She's going to pull through,' he said. 'And we've discovered what caused the adverse reaction.'

'Can it be cured?' she asked.

'I doubt it,' he said, with faint amusement. '"It" turns out to be fifty-seven, female, and totally unaware that she's done anything wrong. Mrs Markham's sister, Winnie,' he explained as Amanda stared at him in utter bewilderment. 'She was so sorry for poor Dorothy, unable to sleep in that big noisy hospital, that she gave her a sleeping tablet she keeps in her handbag.'

Amanda gasped. 'As simple as that?'

Malory nodded. 'Things often are.'

She said stiltedly, 'I'm glad for you. It must be a great weight off your mind. There was a silence, then she said, in a little rush, 'Malory, what am I doing here?'

He walked forward slowly, shrugging off his jacket, loosening his tie. 'You're starting to be a wife to me—in every way there is.'

She shook her head. 'I—I can't. Not while you think I've been unfaithful to you—while you think our baby. . .' Her voice was choked with tears suddenly, and she couldn't go on.

He sat down on the edge of the bed, not touching her. He said, 'When I saw you lying in the road that day, a lot of things suddenly became very clear. I'd sworn, years ago, that I'd never let Nigel get to me again. I thought if he saw that his sordid little games didn't matter to me, then he'd stop. On the whole, I succeeded. But everything changed when I saw you. You were my Achilles' heel, and Nigel knew it. Even before you were engaged, it gave him sadistic pleasure to tell me what it was like to kiss you—to touch your breasts. How I stopped myself from killing him, I'll never know.'

She looked at him in total bewilderment. 'But you didn't know me.'

'I'd never met you,' he said, 'but I'd seen you— at some rally lunch in the Lakes. Nigel had dragged me there, and I was bored out of my skull. Then, across the room, I saw you—a girl with hair like autumn leaves, and virginal eyes.' He gave an uneven laugh. 'I said I didn't believe in instant bliss Well, I didn't believe in love at first sight either, yet there I was, lost, hopelessly and for all eternity. I was on my way to you when I saw Nigel looking at me, then at you. I saw him smile, like the cat that stole the cream, and I stood there, and watched him step in and take you away from me, and there wasn't a damned thing I could do about it.'

'You were there—that day?' Her lips parted soundlessly. 'But I didn't realise . . .'

He smiled at her, putting a hand out to touch her cheek in a fleeting caress. 'I know, my darling.'

'But—if you've loved me all this time, why didn't you tell me?'

'I was terrified I might frighten you away,' he said simply. 'You wanted protection from me, not passion. I thought if I held back, gave you time, you might come to care for me—to give me what I wanted from you.' He sighed briefly. 'When you came to me that afternoon, threw yourself into my arms, I knew it was too soon—but you were so lovely, so totally desirable, I couldn't resist you. And, like some adolescent, I lost my head completely—shocked you—hurt you.'

Colour stole into her face. 'But you made up for that later,' she said in a low voice. 'Why did you walk away from me afterwards?'

'Hurt pride, to some extent,' he admitted grimacing. 'And the conviction that you still weren't ready for the complete sexual commitment I wanted from you. You see, I couldn't get away from the idea that, in your heart, in spite of everything, you still wanted Nigel.'

'Oh, you're so wrong!' Her voice broke. 'Malory, I don't know how to make you believe me, but I began loving you a long time ago, only I just didn't realise it. Then, that day when Nigel came here and he kissed me—it made me see how I really felt.' She shivered. 'When he touched me, I felt sick, dirty, but I didn't fight him in case it made things worse.'

He took her hands in his. 'Amanda, why didn't you tell me he'd been here?'

She gave a little sigh. 'I forgot. It—it just wasn't important enough to remember. All that mattered was you—and letting you know how I felt about you.'

His eyes were tender. 'You have a faultless sense of priority, my sweet, but if you'd mentioned Nigel's visit, even in passing, I'd have been on my guard. As it was, when I opened that envelope, I felt as if I'd been pole-axed—all my worst nightmares coming true at once.' He groaned. 'All my life I've been analysing situations and making logical conclusions, but I can't be rational where you're concerned. I was too hurt and jealous to even consider the possibility that Nigel was up to his old tricks again. All I could remember was that you'd once told me you didn't know if you could trust yourself where Nigel was concerned. I began to think that you'd given yourself to me out of guilt—and it nearly drove me mad.'

He shook his head. 'I'd been out that morning, making arrangements to take you away on a proper honeymoon. On the way back, I'd bought out some florist's for you. The flowers were there on the desk when I opened the photographs. They seemed to be mocking me—telling me what a fool I'd been.'

She said gently, 'You threw them away, didn't you? Mrs Priddy found them, and brought them to me. They made me feel very sad, although I didn't understand why.'

'I shouldn't have left as I did,' he said, 'but I didn't trust myself. I felt I had to get away, lick my wounds in privacy, but it just made everything worse. I kept tormenting myself, seeing you with Nigel—imagining you doing with him what you'd done with me. I thought I'd go crazy, I was hurting so much. I wanted to hurt you in turn, and I did— didn't I?'

She shivered. 'Yes.'

He said slowly, 'I watched you walk away from me, and I thought, what the hell? I love her, and I always will, and even if it isn't my baby, it's part of her, and I'll love it and cherish it for her sake.'

She said passionately, 'Do you think—do you really think I could bear to have any man's child inside me but yours? Oh, God, I love you so much!' She pushed aside the covers, scrambling on to her knees, throwing her arms round his neck and seeking his mouth with frantic ardour.

His arms enclosed her crushingly, and they kissed again and again, desperately, yearningly.

At last he pulled himself away, his breathing ragged. He said, 'Darling, we've got to stop. You need to rest . . .'

'I need you.' Her hands tugged at the buttons of his shirt.

Malory groaned. 'So much for all my virtuous intentions,' he muttered. He lifted her gently, and set her back against the pillows, before starting to take off his clothes. She watched him, savouring the urgent race of her breathing, the clamour of her blood.

He lay beside her and kissed her mouth, then swiftly removed her nightgown, dropping it on the floor beside the bed. 'No more barriers of any kind,' he whispered. His brows drew together as he looked at her. 'My poor, bruised love. I hardly dare touch you.'

She arched against him, loving the naked brush of his skin against her own, drawing his hands to her breasts. 'I'm not that fragile.'

He caressed her with skilful tenderness, his body infinitely gentle as it penetrated hers. The pleasure, when it came, was gentle, too—like a breeze rippling across a field of corn—and so beautiful that it stirred Amanda to her very soul.

He said remorsefully, 'Darling, you're crying. I hurt you . . .'

'No, oh, no!' She pressed small kisses to his face and throat. 'I—I thought that would never happen to me again.'

'No chance.' Malory wrapped her in his arms, kissing the remaining tears away. 'I would never have let you go. If you'd left me, I'd have followed you to the end of the world.'

'You are my world.' She looked at him, her heart in her eyes, and saw her love reflected in his own gaze.

'And now, my pregnant angel, it's time you got some of the sleep the doctor ordered,' he told her firmly.

'On one condition.' She snuggled her cheek against his bare shoulder. 'When I wake in the morning, I want to be in your arms.'

'You will be,' he said. 'In my arms, and in my heart, all the days of our lives.'

And, with a sigh of total contentment, Amanda closed her eyes.

Harlequin American Romance

**Romances that go one step farther...
American Romance**

Realistic stories involving people you can relate to and
care about.

Compelling relationships between the mature men and
women of today's world.

Romances that capture the core of genuine emotions
between a man and a woman.

Join us each month for four new titles wherever paperback
books are sold.
Enter the world of American Romance.